Han Birondo is from the Philippines. She's an HR management professional certified both in Learning & Development Training and Lean Six Sigma. She started writing poetry in 1997 when she first fell in love with a classmate in college. She has written dozens since. She also wrote hundreds of personal quotes borne from personal experiences on life, love and loss which she later published under the title Then Eve Speaks, volumes I – III. This first novel is her memoir for a love that was destined not to be.

For my Sam, thank you for making this dream come true for me.

Han Birondo

OF LOVE AND FAITH

AUSTIN MACAULEY PUBLISHERS™
LONDON • CAMBRIDGE • NEW YORK • SHARJAH

Copyright © Han Birondo 2024

The right of Han Birondo to be identified as author of this work has been asserted by the author in accordance with Federal Law No. (7) of UAE, Year 2002, Concerning Copyrights and Neighboring Rights.

All rights reserved. No part of this publication may be reproduced, stored in a retrieval system, or transmitted in any form or by any means, electronic, mechanical, photocopying, recording, or otherwise, without the prior permission of the publishers.

Any person who commits any unauthorized act in relation to this publication may be liable to legal prosecution and civil claims for damages.

This is a work of fiction. Names, characters, businesses, places, events, locales, and incidents are either the products of the author's imagination or used in a fictitious manner. Any resemblance to actual persons, living or dead, or actual events is purely coincidental.

The age group that matches the content of the books has been classified according to the age classification system issued by the Ministry of Culture and Youth.

ISBN – 9789948761730 – (Paperback)
ISBN – 9789948761747 – (E-Book)

Application Number: MC-10-01-6657725
Age Classification: 17+

Printer Name: iPrint Global Ltd
Printer Address: Witchford, England

First Published 2024
AUSTIN MACAULEY PUBLISHERS FZE
Sharjah Publishing City
P.O Box [519201]
Sharjah, UAE
www.austinmacauley.ae
+971 655 95 202

January 2018 – Present Time

Why do we love? Air and water are essentials to life. Many say so is love. Why?

16 days before he leaves Dubai, and here I am asking myself a fundamental question that has dumbfounded millions of other people across the world. I had experienced the answer to that question, and yet each time my relationships broke down, I stopped and wondered why we love.

I close my eyes, meaning to halt my thoughts. Then the image of his face, with his beautiful green eyes smiling at me, flashes on the screen of my mind. How to escape this? How do you stop thinking of the one person you want to think of all day?

Life had prepared me for the eventuality of his leaving. My mind had let him go some time back. My heart has yet to do so. The pages of my journal hold in secret the grief that's drilling me from within.

Does the heart ever let go?
And how can you let go of someone
you have been waiting for all your life?
How do you stop loving the one person
you want to love all along?

It's a new year, and I should be concentrating on my resolutions. I intend to burn some gained weight on the elliptical machine this afternoon, at the same time as the past days when the gym in my building was empty. Yet here I am, deeply rooted in a chair in a Starbucks coffee shop near the JBR tram station and swimming in my own thoughts. I always find it hard to move physically when I'm heavy with emotions. Feelings are a lot harder to lose than those extra pounds I put on during the holidays, and a lot more difficult to carry around you as they compound. Something that's meant to be shared becomes some kind of burden when you have to keep it all inside you because expressing it would mean crossing a line that's not meant to be crossed. In the absence of my physical journal, my mind makes a mental note of a bugging thought.

Why are there religions? What need do we have for it?

It's two in the afternoon, and I should be getting back to my place. But my confusion glues me on this same chair since nine this morning. I have had a tall serving of green tea, a slice of blueberry cheesecake, and a spicy turkey sandwich, yet I still feel hungry. Or is this emptiness I feel? It's hard for me to determine really. Since our director informed me of Zaki's planned transfer late in September of last year, I seemed to be swinging from one emotion to the next, unable to fully grasp each day that passed since.

My phone vibrates beside my mug. The intrusion slightly startles me. It's a WhatsApp message from one of my girlfriends inviting me to a movie. I don't feel like replying. Even my fingers don't want to move. That's how deeply this matter is affecting me. The pain is as real as my hands, one holding the phone and the other clasping the mug, basking from the heat that's emanating from it. I'm going through the memories of our early days when my phone vibrates again, but continuously this time. I can't ignore Lana. She's the most suspicious of all my friends here in Dubai. She can easily sense my indifference. My index finger, out of respect, slides to the right of the screen and accepts the call.

"Hey, Lana," that's all I could muster. My mouth is refusing to open. My entire body seems to have been crippled by the pain in my heart.

"Hi, girl! Where are you?"

My best friend is asking me where I am. Physically I am in Dubai but the rest of me even I don't know where exactly. I must answer. If I stay quiet, she would put me on a hot chair, and cross-interrogation with the likes of Lana isn't something I need right now.

"Starbucks, in the intersection to JBR, near the tram." It must have taken me too long to answer for her to ask the next question.

"Are you okay? You seem not yourself lately."

There we go. When she asks that, it usually means that she senses something out of the ordinary with me. How best to answer that? I'm not even sure myself if I'm okay.

"Hanna?" Comes her probing.

Speak Hanna! I slightly convulse inside, hearing my own mind shouts at me.

"Yeah, Lana, I'm good."

No, you're not, retorts my brain. *She doesn't have to know. No one has to know. I don't want to explain anything to anyone. This feeling, this love, wasn't forced into my heart. This was something fate had orchestrated. Life planted the seeds and time helped them to grow. And I nourished it along the way.*

"You don't sound like you are. I'm going there. Wait for me." And with that, she cuts off the call. A familiar uneasiness starts to rattle my insides.

Lana is one of my closest and most trusted friends. We met three years ago through a mutual friend and became instant friends ourselves. She has this open and easy way about her that just melts one's defenses. If lovers have soul mates, we are like soul sisters. A few months into our friendship and we already know some intimate details about each other. It's that effortless to unlock yourself to someone like her. Her friendship is refreshing. Her humor has been a great aid in easing the stresses of my daily life here. Not that Dubai is a depressing place to be. It's quite the opposite, actually. Dubai is a beautiful place with many beautiful people, including Zaki. The mere mention of his name causes my heart to flutter. I'm about to daydream, to go back in time to when Zaki and I first met when the cold wind from outside rushes into the café. It momentarily surprises me. Lana steps in with a worried look on her face. My silence has awakened the dragon.

"After I order my coffee, we will talk."

No pleasantries; straight to business. My equilibrium shifts, not that I have actually been balancing these past months.

"So, what's up with you?"

And the inquisition begins as soon as she takes her seat in front of me. I can come up with excuses, but none of them will work with her. Lana has a fourth eye, an eighth sense, and a built-in filter that screens the crap from people, including me. It's best to go with the truth.

"I'm just tired a lot lately."

Well, that's *technically* true. Work had been up to my neck during the last quarter of last year. The reality of Zaki leaving submerged me nose-deep.

"You look more than tired. You seem sad."

Sadness is an understatement. *I'm going through hell.* But there's no way I can tell her that – at least not yet.

"Really?" I want to see how long I can evade her inquiry.

"The usual smile in your eyes is missing. There's something like a cloud around your lids, seemingly heavy with tears."

No, she's not a witch. She just has that ultra-sensitive sensory that can determine facts even when they're not presented. Her words stir me inside. The gates in my eyes can barely able to hold back tears.

"Zaki is leaving for France, for good." My lips are quivering now. There's no point in delaying my surrender. Her unwillingness to let this go would only make her press even more.

"Zaki. Zaki. Zaki. How can I get your mind off this guy? How can I get him out of your system?"

How indeed? Even for a moment, perhaps it will do me good to be able to forget about him. I stay quiet. My mind can't form words into coherent sentences at the moment. It's one thing to be lost in my own thoughts. It's another thing to be with Lana.

"Girl, he's a very old issue. It's 2018."

I'm perfectly aware of the time. Though on most instances when I'm alone, I always get lost and my mind would travel back to 2014.

"Love knows no time, Lana. It has no expiration date." My tears come with that.

"There you go again with your one-liners. Can you repeat that, please? I'll shout it out on my Facebook wall."

I quietly wipe the tears, paying her no thought.

"When is he leaving?" She turns serious again as she sees me looking somber.

"23rd," I'm forcing the words out of my mouth.

"Good. The sooner, the better. You deserve more, girl. He's not a loss."

I wonder why we always have to say that to our friends. I don't understand the point of why we have to demean the one who breaks – unintentionally for some – the hearts of our friends.

If he's not my loss, then what is this emptiness that is gnawing inside me?

"Stop thinking about him, Hanna. Don't waste your energy any more than you already have."

The only way for that to be possible is if I would have brain surgery – literally, for the surgeon to extract my brains out of my skull. For no matter what I'm doing, his thoughts have a way of creeping into my consciousness. It has enough authority to command me to stop. No, this is not an obsession. I love him. I love Zaki so much.

"You need to see other guys. That's one effective way to forget him."

"Not now, Lana," my voice lost its edge. I don't have to feign strength with her.

"Then when? You've been on this for years now. You have to help yourself move on, girl. There's no future with him."

How painful it may be to hear that, Lana is right. We have no future, but my journal bears the record of a past that can never be forgotten.

I may never understand why we had to meet,
but I'm thankful that we did.
Yes, we may not have a future,
but we had memories, moments we shared together.
For that I'll forever be grateful for nonetheless.

Chapter 1

June 2013

I must leave. I need to get out of here. I need to be someplace else.

That's how I was when CNN went for commercial breaks. I couldn't stop myself from thinking. Every day it's the same thought – leaving. But where should I go? I didn't have an unending supply of funds to see me through my escapades until I realized where I must be. My phone vibrated on my lap. It was Lourdes. Those days, I didn't want to be asked how I was, because I honestly didn't have a straight answer to give. I was perplexed by the constant thought of leaving the country. I had noted down – mentally – concrete reasons why I should go, but explaining that to another person seemed more daunting than making someone understand how the tsunami in Japan happened. I ignored her message. It could wait. It's my rest day. My phone vibrated again. It's another message from Lourdes asking me when I would come. I rolled my eyes in slight irritation. She didn't live in the next city anymore. It's not like I could just get into a taxi and go to her. I tossed my phone to the other end of the couch.

Later. Right now, I must think. Where to go?

Then, as if an answered prayer, there on the television a tourism advertisement about Dubai. *What a coincidence! Lourdes is in Dubai.* The commercials were over, and Becky Anderson was back, continuing on with the headlines. I was not in our living room anymore, at least mentally.

Dubai. The name itself became very interesting right then. There was England, Australia, India, Cambodia, Japan, Germany, France, the USA, Egypt, Spain, and many other countries I knew and had studied about in school. *Dubai.* I had never given it much thought. I fired open the laptop. During my days off back then I hardly talked to people, but I had my "necessities" near me.

United Arab Emirates. Middle East. My internal alarm lit up inside me. I had been following on television the situation in the Middle East since 2011. The Arab Spring was moving and causing destruction on its trail. The UAE wasn't so far off from the seat of chaos. I may be bored being in the Philippines, but my idea of adventure, of something new, wasn't war or anything even remotely close to it. I closed the laptop. I turned off the television. Then I closed my eyes. There are over 195 countries in the world. Surely there should be someplace better. *Define better?* Sometimes my habit of talking to myself could go out of hand. Days on end, I could just be in my room, not talking to anyone, even with my brother and mom. But during those times, the conversations were taking place inside my head – with me. What could I expect in Dubai? *Let's find out.*

I reached for my phone and lay down on the couch. The internet was a very good source of information. I opted to first watch documentaries about the city and about the country. It seemed like a really nice place to go to. Since it opened its doors, people from all over the world had come to its shores, carrying with them their cultures, traditions, and dreams. Dubai was described as a cosmopolitan city in all of the Gulf region by one British television anchor who filmed an episode on his program about the Emirate. *But is it safe there?* I closed my eyes and turned on the screen inside my head. The Arab Spring had already covered most parts of the Middle East. I was connecting each country with a dot, beginning in Tunisia when a male vendor lit himself on the streets in 2011. The smoke from his burning body reached many areas of the Arab peninsula, so to speak. There were civil unrests in Morocco, Libya, and Egypt, and the situation in Syria was worsening by the day, affecting the economy and lives of its neighboring countries. Iraq was still on the red flag. Saudi Arabia was at a standstill, weighing carefully the crises on its borders and beyond. There were concerns in the southern part too, as Yemen seemed to have been affected by the fever rising in the region. *And the UAE?* That's one advantage of having an active mind; there's direction in my thoughts. I researched about the UAE – economic standing, traditions, cultures, and general way of life. As per a recent study, the country was teeming with expats, with their population bigger than that of the locals. Jobs were available, and more were being generated as investors were coming in because of the no-tax policy enforced. That sounded very good to me.

It's time for Geography. With the ever-present threat of war on its doors, I shouldn't be complacent about safety. Manila to Dubai would be eight and a half hours on a straight flight. China and Hong Kong could be two of the options for connecting flights. Oman and Qatar would be good alternatives as well if the flag carriers from either country would be one's choice for traveling. England would just be six and a half hours travel from Dubai. It's turning out to be a very promising destination for me.

*

November 2013

"You're going to where?" I didn't say Iraq or Afghanistan, so I didn't understand why Molly seemed very surprised.

"I want to go to Dubai. I'm not as decided yet, though," I said dryly. Most of the time, I preferred to keep things to myself, primarily because I didn't like being assaulted with questions.

"But why Dubai? What's there, and what are you going to do there?" And so it goes. I was sure there were more to come. I should have kept my mouth shut.

"I don't know, Molly."

"So why go there?" Good question. I couldn't answer it just yet. There's just this strangeness inside me telling me to go there.

"Change. I want change."

"Oh my gee!" She seemed very concerned all of a sudden.

"What?" It's my turn to be surprised.

"Is everything okay, Hanna?" Her question didn't register with me immediately. I gave her a quizzical look.

"Why out of the blue you just want to leave everything behind and move somewhere else?"

Does one have to be torn apart inside just for wanting to move to another place? Wasn't the desire for change enough motivation to go?

"I'm bored here," that's as honest as I could go. "Come on. Our break is almost over."

I stood abruptly and motioned Molly to follow me out of the pantry. If I allowed the conversation to go on, I might be swayed to change my mind. *My life, my choices.* I should have the right to live it as I see fit, even if that would mean living in another country. *But are you sure about Dubai?* Sometimes I wondered if other people's minds were as active as mine. *Am I sure about Dubai? No. But has there been anyone sure about anything at all?*

Back at our desks, Molly started on her talk show-like approach when she was trying to squeeze information from me.

"Is there something you're not telling me, Hanna?" Molly's round eyes were concentrated on me, her face displaying genuine concern.

"What made you think so, Molly?"

"I don't know, Hanna, but it seems that way with you lately."

I looked at her blankly.

"I notice how restless you are these days. You always seem to be thinking."

"But I'm always thinking, Molly."

"Yes, but there seems to be something different with your aura lately. I can't say exactly what is going on with you. I just know that you're going through something nowadays. I have been wanting to ask you. I didn't know how to bring it up until now."

Molly and I had known each other since 2006. Our shared values and political ideologies made us bond faster than one turned a page of a daily broadsheet. Her suspicion of my hidden thoughts didn't surprise me.

"The thought of leaving has been constant in my mind, and as the days go on, it just seems to get stronger."

"Okay. But how did you come up with Dubai? It's in a Muslim country."

"I have two good friends who are working there. One of them has been inviting me for years to come. And I don't know, Molly, but after seeing an ad on TV about Dubai, I just couldn't stop thinking about it."

"That's your typical reaction to things that interest you. You grow passionate about things and places that pique your curiosity."

"But there seems to be something more to it, Molly. I can't put a grip on it as yet. I'm sure, though, that this is more than just mere fascination."

"Hanna – "

"Like there's something waiting for me there."

"Not something, but someone. *Perhaps he is there*," the conviction in her voice was different. It alarmed me instantly.

"Who?" My heart was starting to beat faster.

"*The one for you*." Her face conveyed the resoluteness I heard in her voice. The sweet uneasiness inside me was growing by the minute. My mind couldn't protest against the idea. In fact, it seemed to be extending two arms to embrace the thought.

"You had stopped dating for a long time, so the thought of meeting someone there surprised you now." She was right again. I smiled in response.

In the taxi on the way home, I was still thinking about what Molly said. All these time reading entries online and watching videos on YouTube about Dubai I hadn't thought, surprisingly, even once, about meeting someone, a man particularly. Since my last break up, in 2008, I became preoccupied with my self-enhancement and my own happiness, cliché as it may sound. I had read 300 books – from the children's classic Rumpelstiltskin, the contemporary works of Paulo Coelho to the educational Almanac of World History – this one cover to cover, right through to a more celebrity piece like the autobiography of David Beckham. Of course, my greatest preoccupation was about the history of the ancient Egyptians. I had exhausted YouTube videos to watch about ancient Egypt. Apart from that, I had watched 67 movies online and in the cinema. I had watched over and over Keanu Reeves' movies. I had traveled within my country from north to south, visiting 113 main islands in total. I wasn't trying to escape the pain. I was trying to cope, living life with a different approach. And now here I was, once more beset with thoughts of love. I couldn't say that I didn't miss the company of a man, the feeling of holding a man's hand, of kissing a man. But I have had it all before. It made me happy, but it also nearly shattered me. It's a traumatizing experience. I didn't wish to go over it again.

My phone vibrated, breaking the flow of thoughts in my mind. It's an SMS from Jinky, my best friend since college.

Jinky: Hanna, are you free to meet tomorrow?
Me: Sure. Just let me know what time and where.

I told Jinky about my intention to leave the country and settle in Dubai. Like Molly, she expressed alarm over the idea. Apart from my personal safety, I believed that my friends were more concerned about my emotional state. I never said anything about my last breakup since when it happened. I had not gone out with anyone again, nor had I expressed a desire to do so. I was 30 years old, had a loving family, shared strong friendships with wonderful women my age, and I was financially stable. What would I need a man for?

"Who will look after you there?" I may not have been lucky with men, but I was blessed with awesome friends. Jinky, though younger than me by one year, was admonishing me like an older sister.

"I can take care of myself now. No need to worry, Jinky." It's hard to put strength in my words in between mouthful servings of the tasty Sisig we ordered.

"Why all of a sudden you thought of leaving? And why Dubai? It's in a Muslim country." Her remark was similar to that of Molly's. As if there was something frightening about the Muslims that they both had to remind me of it. But I think it was natural for people to be skeptical over matters they had little understanding about.

"I've been thinking about this for months now. It seems like a really good choice for me."

"What did your family say?"

"There was an initial shock, especially from Mom. But I think I can convince them to allow me to go. After all, I would come back home should things not turn out well for me there."

"Your other brother is in England. Why not go there instead?" Jinky wasn't showing signs that she was willing to let this go my way.

"I want to be on my own, Jinky. I want to know how to live alone and fend for myself. I'm 30 years old. There's only a very small part of life I have seen and experienced. I want more."

"Is there something that you're not telling me, Hanna?" I had to laugh at that, which surprised her. "What's funny about it?"

"My other best friend from work had asked me yesterday exactly the same question." I was trying to stifle my laugh.

"Well, obviously we're both very concerned for you." She didn't look amused.

"Okay, I'm sorry. I meant no disrespect. Just that I had been asked the same question two days in a row."

"Well, are you keeping anything from me?"

"No, I'm not, Jinky. I have nothing to keep from you, and there's no reason to, if ever. But I just want to leave and be somewhere else now. I want to experience life in another country. I want something new."

"But why Dubai? Where did you get the idea to go there?" I knew that her worries stem from the recent news involving Muslims in the southern part of our country. People were so quick to believe in the media and form their opinions of others from what they watched.

"I saw it on TV one time. I researched about it. The place seems very promising. I have the potential to earn a lot. Plus, two of my good friends are there too."

"Hanna, are you leaving the country so you can forget and move on?" I had been waiting for that. Still, it took me a moment to answer.

"Jinky, I had moved on. I'm alright. I hadn't forgotten a thing about what happened, but I don't think that I need to either. What happened had happened, and it had taught me a great deal. But it's not the reason why I'm leaving. I just don't want to be here anymore. I want something new for my life. I promised that I'd look after myself very well. Please don't worry so much," I said it with utmost earnestness. I reached out for her hands. Her tears drew out mine too.

*

January 2014

"Are you sure?" There's that question again. I had to give an affirmative answer, or I would never even get to the airport.

"Lourdes is there. My former officemate and good friend, Carol, also lives there with her family. I should be okay."

"Call the soonest you arrive. If things do not happen as you planned, come home."

My older brother, Hector, was one of my sweetest gifts from God. He's ever so loving and supportive. He and my other older brother, Henry, had pampered me with attention, love, and material things growing up. But I was an adult already, a complete woman. It's time to be independent of their care, time to live life outside of their protection. It's time to be on my own. Dubai was waiting.

"How will you survive on your own when you don't even know how to boil an egg?" My mother was beyond worried.

"I'll be fine, Mom." I could fool the world with my confidence, but not my own mother. She wasn't buying my words.

"What if you get sick? When you get an asthma attack from the heat there, what then?"

Her voice signaled the coming of tears. A string was pulled in my heart just then. I had no insurance independent of the one I used to have with my former company. I didn't see the point in getting one now since I had no plans to return here except for vacations. *I will make it.* I wished I could manifest in my voice the assurance I felt inside. But regardless of how good I was with words, sometimes I failed to verbalize myself.

"Mom, please don't worry so much. I'll look after myself."

What I failed to express in words, I made up through my actions. I hugged my mother tightly, hoping that the certainty I held in my heart could penetrate hers and somehow ease the negativity I filled it with. I knew that no amount of words could put a break on her tears at the moment. Making it right on my own in Dubai would give validation for her unhappiness. I made a quiet resolution in my heart to do whatever I could to prove to her that this decision would bring rewarding aftermaths to make up for the heavy feeling I was leaving her behind with.

*

March 2014

Three days before my flight to Dubai, I met up with the mother of my late friend, Cielo. Together, we went to the cemetery, where she was laid to rest.

How do you let go of someone who has already left?

My hand couldn't write any more than that. I couldn't stop my tears. She had been dead for one year now. I wouldn't even have known about it had it not been for a Facebook post her niece put on her wall and which I saw on my feeds. We lost touch. I got busy with work, with my own life. In short, I became selfish for some time, not minding my friends much. I knew she was sick that's why she came back home. The last time we spoke, she was in remission from her cancer on the lymph nodes. I asked her to keep me abreast of her condition. But I should have been the one who should have made the follow-up. The guilt had sharp nails, burrowing inside my heart.

I am sorry, Cielo. I miss you so much.

That afternoon's experience was both sad and painful, yet there was a sense of liberation to it as well. I didn't know how to explain it. The heart sometimes seemed to understand faster than the mind – at least mine did. I didn't want to complicate the feeling and decided instead to just allow it to fill me.

Be with me, Cielo. Walk with me in Dubai.

I cried a bit more. I rolled over to the side of my bed to get a tissue from the drawer. For no apparent reason, I thought of opening the bottom tier. My old red wallet was inside. I picked it up and was surprised to see one Dirham coin in the purse. The tears were coming again, meaningful and sweet tears. Cielo gave it to me on her first vacation back to the country from her initial trip to Dubai. I took that as a sign of affirmation from her.

14 March 2014

Eight and a half hours after traveling through the clouds, the wind helped me reach Dubai International Airport,

Terminal 1. It was 23 minutes past the hour of 11 in the evening, local time. I breezed through immigration, and my luggage came out quicker than I had expected. Even the line for the taxi was short. I was assigned a lady driver with a pink cab, which amused me. I had never been in one similar to it before. I gave her the name of my hotel located in Tecom. She's a confident driver, racing on the wide roads. We arrived at the hotel in just over 30 minutes. The attendant at the front desk was a charming young man, not more than 26 years old, I supposed, with long lashes flickering constantly with those beautiful brown eyes. From the airport to here, so far, all was good. When I got to my suite I was mesmerized with the interiors. I loved the intricate designs on the carpet, both in the living area and in my bedroom. The design of the bed headboard fascinated me. It looked like a window – to a new world I was eager to discover. For months, the thought of coming here occupied my mind day and night. I imagined walking on the streets of Dubai, inhaling the desert air, and filling my lungs with the breath of its success. And now here I was. I was shedding tears of relief and triumph. *New beginning, new dreams, new life.* I was filled with excitement at the prospect of new experiences, of the growth this place could offer me, and of the transformations my life would have.

After a warm shower, I headed to bed. The lamp hanging in the corner of the room caught my attention. I fixated on it while lying down. It's similar to stained-glass windows in churches. It had vibrant colors. The shape was like an inverted dome of a mosque, with the tip pointing down. It's beautiful. I had never seen anything like it. I knew there were many more like that I would see here. I couldn't wait to see them all! I closed my eyes, and a sense of accomplishment washed over me. *I'm here. I'm in Dubai.* I had no grand illusions about making it big here. I was certain, however, that I could be more than I was back home. Deciding to work and live abroad was one of the boldest decisions I had ever made in my life so far. I felt proud of myself. But in split seconds, I felt another emotion, almost as intense – fear. Tomorrow I would wake up away from my mother and brother in a different world I knew little about. All my months of reading about Dubai and the UAE, and even about the region, I knew might not suffice to prepare me for what I might actually experience here. I felt compelled to pray. Sleepiness won over me shortly after I closed my benediction.

*

I was awakened by the phone screaming on the bedside table. I answered with a coarse voice.

"Hello."

"Good morning, babe!" An enthusiastic Lourdes was on the other line.

"Hi, babe. You woke me up. What time is it?" In an instant, I remembered that I wasn't home anymore. I stood abruptly, dropping the receiver on the floor, and I rushed to the window to peek through what was outside. *Yes, I'm really here!* My lips curved into a smile, and I giggled. *Oh my, Lourdes!*

"Hello? Babe, I'm sorry. I didn't mean that," excitement was evident in my voice.

"I'm coming over. Let's have breakfast," she said, equally excited. She had been inviting me for years to come to Dubai.

The bug's bite finally hit me deep enough this time, so to speak. I took a quick shower, then unzipped my luggage for fresh clothes. A beaming Lourdes gave me a tight squeeze the moment she saw me.

"Welcome to Dubai!"

"I finally made it. Thanks for the push." I really was grateful that she had pressed on through the years for me to come. There's a certain beat to this place that's so enticing for me, despite the fact that I had only been here for less than 24 hours.

"How was your flight? We should go to the Dubai Mall. There's a huge bookstore there."

"Oh, I'm very pleased to know that." My whole being was electrified at the moment. My feet were itchy, and my eyes were eager to behold the wonders in this city.

"Where will you be staying?"

"With my friend Carol in DIP. Do you know where that is?"

"Dubai Investment Park. That's somewhere near the outskirts of Dubai, on the side going to Abu Dhabi."

"Far from here, then?"

"It is, a bit. Perhaps it would take you 20 minutes maximum going there by taxi. I'm not sure of the bus routes. But on the weekends, you can stay with me."

"Let the fun begin!" And we made a high five.

Apart from my good friend, Carol, there's no one else I could imagine being here with over than Lourdes. We had known each other since our days at Citibank, some ten years back. She was one of those I got along so easily with. She had a depth to her that I like. Her disdain for superficiality and celebrity gossip was on the same level as mine. All girls love talking about men, and the two of us were no exception. However, our conversations did not revolve around them alone. She's the only one amongst my friends with whom I could talk about politics and religion for hours. She's never bothered if I read the newspapers instead of talking to her while we were waiting for our food when dining out.

"You'll be busy here, dating guys from one country to the next!"

Guys. My, I hadn't thought of that. I had been solely focused on the economic and geopolitical matters of the country and in the region.

"Yes. I learned that there are people from more than 150 countries in this Emirate alone." I felt a sudden jolt inside. The same kind of strangeness I had experienced when I first saw the advertisement for Dubai last year.

"You'll not be bored here. I'm sure you'll meet someone in no time."

Well, that might be inevitable, but it wasn't the reason why I came. Change.

Could the heart be capable of that too?

"Can we go back to my room? I need to call Carol. I will be checking out shortly."

Better to cut short any discussion on men sooner, or else my heart would dwell on the subject for longer than needed. I should stay focused. I left my family, the comforts of home, and the warm company of good friends for this. I must not fail.

Chapter 2

The roads were wide and winding. My dizziness was growing with each turn on each roundabout. The coziness of Carol's home made up for my discomfort on the way, though. I felt right at home so fast. My first few days were spent with introduction to their friends and attending simple family picnics and gatherings. I warmed up to their circle immediately enough, passed the usual pleasantries. By the day my resolution for staying here in Dubai was gaining strength. It looked like I could really have a new life here. But first, I needed a job.

Carol called home one afternoon as I was reading to her kids. She said I should expect a call from an international company that was looking to hire an executive assistant for the managing director and as general office administrator for their branch here in Dubai. I was surprised and quiet for a moment. She sensed my confusion and explained that she had applied for me.

"But where did you get my CV?"

"I just passed your name and number to my friend who's working there. Just prepare one now. They might invite you over for an interview."

True enough, in an hour's time, the phone rang again. It's an agent from a recruiting firm representing the searching company. She's asking basic questions. I volunteered to send her an updated CV. She said she would call again sometime after receiving it. Upon putting the receiver down, I went to work on my resumé. I felt somewhat uncomfortable.

I was serving the kids their afternoon snacks when the phone rang once more just a couple of hours after. It's the same lady. I was asked to come the following day between 11 in the morning to four in the afternoon for an interview. My heartbeat was racing by the time the call ended. It wasn't the interview that I dreaded. I could sit down with the Secretary General of the UN any time, and I wouldn't even shed a sweat. *Then what's this uneasiness about?* I didn't know just yet. Not all answers would come to us when we wanted them, which frustrated me just by thinking about it.

*

Dubai Investment Park (DIP) to Jumeirah Lakes Towers (JLT) was approximately just 20 minutes by taxi. My heart got there faster, though. It wasn't overexcitement. It wasn't fear, either. It's the same feeling one had when something was about to happen, yet one didn't know what, how, or even when it's going to occur. There's a part of me that could sense it but my mind couldn't find the logical explanation for it. And it's frustrating for me when I couldn't determine what that something was. I liked to be always in control of myself, my thoughts, and my feelings. I wanted to be able to predict how things were going to turn out in order for me to be prepared for any losses or pain, be more determined on the best course of action to take to defend myself from either one or know beforehand the best time for me to pull away so as not to experience any of it.

I calmed myself on the way up to the floor where the office was located. The lady who opened the door was the friend that Carol spoke to me about. The office job was boring for her. Her physical appearance and aura explained this to me. She had the built meant for the outdoors. While I was perfectly alright to just sit in front of the computer for eight hours in an air-conditioned office.

After the PRO briefed me on the responsibilities and demands of the job, she endorsed me to the managing director or the boss. The interview lasted for 30 minutes. He liked me and hired me on the spot. I was happy, but all along, the feeling of uneasiness had never left me. In fact, strangely enough, it seemed to be growing and deepening as I was signing the pages of my employment contract. In my heart, I felt like as though I was signing up for more than work.

The weekend went by slowly, much to my dismay. I was eager to come to the office, as if there was something – or someone even – waiting for me there that couldn't wait.

Finally, Sunday came and I got up early. I caught the first bus trip to Ibn Battuta, and from there I took the Metro and got off at JLT. Upon stepping out I walked toward my left in the direction of my new office. I used Lourdes' building residence as my point of reference, which was in the cluster on the right side of the station. The sun was mad so early in the day. I decided to walk through the basements of each building, moving from one cluster to the next. I reached the office 45 minutes after eight, just right for a nine AM call time. I rang the bell. When it opened, I was ushered into a world unlike anything I had imagined, nor was I prepared enough to walk in on.

There standing in front of me, holding the door open, was a man who I had only seen then, but in an instant, I felt like I had known him somewhere back in time, when exactly I didn't know. He stopped me dead at my tracks. He seemed to have been frozen in time, too. For a minute, we were just standing by the door, looking at each other; no words were exchanged. My tongue decided not to work that morning. He blinked and smiled first. Only then that I realized that I had not blinked since getting caught by his eyes! I extended my right hand and introduced myself. He took it and did the same.

"I'm Zaki." Strange, but his voice echoed inside me in a similar fashion when one struck the bell in the church, the sound of it traveling through the walls of my ears and cascaded to my throat, then hitting my ribcages and causing an unexpected jolt in my heart.

I went on to explain that it was my first day there. He was surprised. He didn't know yet that the current director's assistant had resigned. He just arrived that morning from a business trip in India. Good that he thought of coming to work early. Otherwise, I would be waiting outside until someone arrived. Who knew how long that would take.

Have I not been accustomed to waiting?

I surprised myself with that thought. He seemed to sense my hesitancy that's created by such a sudden outburst of thought.

"Is everything okay?"

"Yes. A thought just came to me. It wasn't expected."

"What a thought it must have been! Your cheeks are flashing."

"Oh…It's from the heat outside."

And you, I almost added.

"Well, if you want to freshen up, the ladies' washroom is right on the left."

"Thank you."

"You're welcome – and I meant that in both ways."

And he smiled, showing me his perfect teeth. Then he walked back to his office. I thought of checking myself in the washroom. As he had remarked, my cheeks were flashed. Though I couldn't be certain then what exactly caused it – the heat outside or him. *Him?* I slightly shook hearing my own voice in my head.

I'll think about this later.

I hardly used make-up, so there's no way to hide the redness. I was about to step out when I caught a glimpse of my eyes in the mirror. There's an unfamiliar look to it. It seemed to be *twinkling*, for the lack of a better way to describe it right then. I found myself a bit confused by this, though I wasn't feeling uncomfortable. As much as I would like to continue delving into my own thoughts, I had to concentrate on what lay ahead for today. I said a simple prayer as a way to pacify myself. This outrageous thing – outrageous because it wasn't normal for me – could wait until I would be home tonight and cloak under the privacy of the dark while on my bed.

Josephine oriented me with the basics of the post first. As we progressed through the week, she explained all my administrative functions – from managing the director's office to the internal affairs of the team and general reception, plus supervision of the entire facilities. It's quite a workload but doable. It would make me busy and prevent me from thinking of men, relationships, or love.

Why can you not think of any of it? I was astonished at myself for asking this question, and yet I couldn't seem to hate myself for doing so.

As weeks went by, there had been some surprises, little or trivial they may seem, yet perplexed my mind, like my self-consciousness for one. Since my first day, I had been feeling uneasy in the office. We were a multi-racial team, yet we got along very well. The feeling of newness was short-lived. I integrated myself fast with the group. But I was maniacally aware of how distant I was inside. I was on full alert, so to speak. As if I was anticipating an attack and bracing myself well for it, from whom or what I didn't know. I just knew I had to be on guard. At night, I tried to think about it, tried to bring it out in the open, but to no avail. I used to think that darkness was my most honest ally, but right now it seemed to be a great aid in keeping this matter a mystery to me.

One weekend I was in a contemplative mood – meaning I was awfully quiet. Carol had noticed it and asked if everything was alright in the office. Our true friends could always hear what we couldn't say aloud.

"Everything is okay at work. I'm going about it just right." I wished to put more energy into my words to sound more convincing. But I failed.

"Then how come you are so quiet of late? What's bothering you?"

Whenever I was going through something and my mind was processing the matter, my lips were usually sealed. I was aware that it made people wonder, even my friends who had known me for long. But my tongue wouldn't move when my mind couldn't put a hand on what was going on inside me.

"To be frank, I don't know." Carol shot me a questioning look. "There's something going on inside me. A thought keeps pressing itself into my consciousness, like a worm running around in me, causing me to itch in every inch it has passed on. I have been trying to catch it, but it keeps slipping through my fingers. I can't explain it."

"Perhaps the thought is not in your head but in your heart."

A thought in my heart?
How could that be?
What could it be?

What I couldn't ask Carol openly, I expressed with sincerity in my journal. But I hated it when I got lost in the riddle of my own thoughts – or feelings. *But for who?* I hadn't met anyone since coming here. The only interactions I had with men were those from the office. Surely it wasn't possible to develop feelings toward no one in particular.

"Maybe it's not a romantic feeling for anyone, but fear. You're afraid to develop any feelings for anyone," Kaycee, one of our commercial coordinators, said during lunch one day. While that may be true, I sensed there was something more.

*

Weeks past and with the help of work and online movies, thanked heavens for the fast internet connection here in Dubai,

I managed to put aside my bothersome and directionless thoughts.

However, one lazy weekend afternoon, while floating in the pool and basking in the sun, the thought came back without invitation. Panic gripped me when suddenly the image of Zaki showed up on the screen in my mind. I waded clumsily into the water. *Goodness Hanna!* I was standing in the middle of the pool, shaking with a growing confusion. I looked around. I was alone. I swam to the ladder and walked to the lounger. I felt cold – inside. I buried my face in my towel. I was still shaking.

Why? What is this?

"What's going on?" My voice was muffled, with my face still buried in the towel on my hand. I felt tears banging on my lids. I allowed it. I was thinking that perhaps the tears would bring me answers, which then could make me understand.

A good ten minutes passed. The tears gave me relief. I had not cried like that in a long time. It was an emotional release, but mentally baffling.

Why did I cry?

Then my lips moved on their own. "Zaki." Odd as it may seem to me, the sound of his name created a soothing sensation inside me, like the soft light that was emanating from a candle, lighting my dark corners, from which my ignored infatuation for him had been growing.

In the six months since I joined the company, Zaki and I had grown considerably close. We had not gone out on a date. Our time together had always been inside the office. He would be hanging around my desk when he was taking a break and would just ask me whatever question popped into his mind. He seemed genuinely curious about the Philippines and my mixed origins. I, on the other hand, had a deep fascination for Egypt. I knew their ancient history, but I had a lot to catch up on in their current affairs. So our conversations moved from one time period to the next, one country to the other. On some nights, Thursdays usually, we stayed in the office longer after work and chased each other like kids around the conference room or playing our own version of hide and seek – one of us hid an object and the other tried to find it. There's a consequence, of course, if one of us failed to locate the hidden object. I lose all the time. Our game was very physical. There was no social boundary between us. He freely invaded my space, even in front of our colleagues. Strangely enough, none of them seemed to mind our closeness. From my perspective, there's nothing to mind. We were friends. I felt an unusual uneasiness from that thought.

Are we really just friends?

I was starting to lose my footing with my own thoughts again. I wondered how many people could sit with themselves and endure such an inquisition from their own minds. Yes, we're just friends – if the status of our relationship was the one to be considered. But our feelings, my feelings in particular, I realized now that perhaps there's more to it than I cared to admit or had ever considered.

Inside the elevator, on the way up to the apartment, I couldn't look at my reflection on the mirrored walls. I felt somewhat shy, having recognized my feelings toward Zaki. Under the shower, thoughts were running in my mind, but with no particular direction. *Zaki*. I wondered where he was, what he was doing, and with whom. I always meant to ask how his weekends had been on Sundays, but his nearness always absorbed me, making me lose focus.

Where's my blow dryer? I never blew dry my hair during the weekends so as to give it a break. But I liked the sound coming from it because it blocked out all the other sounds around me. And for some odd reason, it helped me to think.

What now? On Sunday, how is it going to be?

I wasn't exactly sure what I was worrying about. For years, I managed to evade love. I hadn't experienced its thrills, but I had peace of mind. Now my thoughts were disturbed and shuffling back and forth like my hair as I continued to dry it.

Am I in love? Hopefully not.

After being hurt in the past, it's scary and difficult for me to fall in love again. Even the thought of it made me back out. But love had a way of curving your path to go in the direction where it would intertwine with that of someone else. And when we made an attempt to untangle ourselves from it, it would pull us in even more. I wasn't certain I wanted to be pulled deeper into this.

I need a book. No better way to divert my thoughts than by reading. If I didn't give much attention to these thoughts, they would lose their bearing and disappear from my mind. *I don't have new books to read!* This momentarily depressed me. How could I have allowed myself to run out of books to read? In six months, I read only seven books. It wasn't like me. Panic rose to my throat like bile. I started to pace in the house. Good thing Carol and her family were out to church. I would be causing her worry if she saw me like this.

What had I been up to in the last months? My journal was almost empty, so I had nothing to refer to. What had I been doing? I closed my eyes and the image of his face flashed in the screen of my mind again. *Zaki*. The thought that I had fallen for him shook me inside out. Leaning on the counter by the kitchen, I opened my phone and looked at our pictures. I didn't realize until today how many pictures we had taken since my first month in the company. I took a closer look at him. There's nothing extraordinary about his face. His green eyes rimmed with dark brown long lashes were not unusual for Egyptians – and there were a good number of them here in Dubai. His chiseled face with pronounced cheekbones was also a common trait of men from this region. Those full lips were neither the most sensuous for I had seen very good-looking Arab men in Dubai Mall who had lips that could rival those of Angelina Jolie. So what was it about Zaki, then? As if to answer me, my phone was vibrating with the incoming call from him.

"Hello, Zaki," there's tentativeness in my voice.

"Hanna, are you okay?" He sounded worried which made me worry too. Had my feelings traveled all the way to him without me realizing it? Was it possible to teleport feelings too?

"Ye… yes, Zaki. I'm okay. How about you?" I hated myself for sounding unsure.

"You sound a bit off, Hanna. I noticed how quiet you were the past week as well."

What? As my mind was cramming for an answer, I felt a tug in my heart with what he said. *He didn't just see me. He could see through me.* This sensitivity was something I couldn't recall having experienced before with any man, even with those I have had relationships with.

"I'm just tired. There's nothing out of the ordinary with me."

Nothing out of the ordinary because falling in love is as natural as breathing. I was taken aback with my own thoughts.

"Do you need anything? What made you call?" This call was stirring me inside even more.

"Ah yeah, just to tell you that I need tickets for Saudi Arabia. I need to leave tomorrow. Do you think you can coordinate with the travel agency today for it?"

"Of course. What time will you be back?"

"On Tuesday. There's a flight with Saudi Air at four in the afternoon. Please book that for me."

"Okay. I'll come back to you shortly for an update."

I still had the phone to my ear even after the call had ended, as if I wanted to stay in that conversation, continue it, and talk about other things. *Zaki.* I closed my eyes with the phone on my lips.

Does he feel the same way?

The thought of seeing him was what helped me overcame the bed this morning. But then I remembered that Zaki flew to Dammam yesterday for business meetings. He would be out of the office for three days. This saddened me. Yet on the other hand, it sorts of offered relief. It's like buying me time – *for what*? Confronting myself with my own infatuation for Zaki was one thing. The thought of seeing him again after my self-admission caused me discomfort, though oddly enough, I didn't dislike it. It heated me up inside, making me aware of the blood that coursed through my veins.

*

When the mind's busy time didn't exist. I was on the phone listening to a customer's request for one product information when Zaki walked in and gave me a wink as he headed in the direction of his office. When I placed the receiver down, I immediately checked my presence table. I was surprised to realize that it was already Wednesday. I panicked all too suddenly. I felt my cheeks turning crimson from the heat that was coursing through my body. I was breathing slowly and mindfully, eyes closed. A minute after I smelled him in the air. Then I felt the softness of his lips on my right cheek. I couldn't move right away. I was accustomed to Zaki's presence near or beside me. But he had never kissed me. It's raising my temperature.

"Hi!" I looked up to him with a smile. He's sitting at my desk. "How was your trip?" He was quiet and was just looking at me. "What?" My voice shrilled the air.

"Your cheeks are so red, Hanna." And he pinched my right cheek.

"It's like that when I'm tense."

What? I openly admitted my own predicament.

"What are you tense about? Did something happen while I was away?" There's genuine concern in his voice. The look on his face backed this up. This utter concern for me, his attentiveness, his sensitivity to *me* – it's all clear to me now. These were what had pulled me closer and closer to him all this time. No one had given me this much attention in the past. Either I was a genius at keeping myself together despite what was happening to me or the people around me back in the Philippines were insensitive to my pain; I couldn't recall any man paying me this much importance.

"Work had been up to my neck. The boss is traveling to the head office again next week. I'm helping him with some reports and presentations," I said matter-of-factly, avoiding looking at his eyes directly.

"Well, it's almost the weekend. You can relax." And he gently massaged my right shoulder before he walked back to his office. My sanity was on the brink of splitting in two.

"Hanna?" My boss' voice startled me back to reality.

"Yes, sir?"

"Are you alright? Your cheeks are very red."

"Just a bit tense about the reports, sir. I'll send it over to you now. Do you mind checking it and let me know if something needs to be changed?"

"You have always been thorough, Hanna. I trust you." And he patted me on the back.

"Thank you, sir." I managed to smile at him.

"Now, go get yourself some ice cream and forget about the reports." He retreated back into his office after reassuring me with his customary clip smile.

I went into the ladies' washroom to check my face. Indeed, I looked like a walking tomato with Chinese eyes. What could I do?

Leave it be and let love.

My eyes grew in bewilderment at such a thought. Where did that come from? Just as when I was considering washing my face, I heard Zaki's voice calling me.

"Yes, Zaki?" I peeked out the door.

"What are you doing hiding in the washroom?"

"I'm not hi…"

"Are you sick? Your cheeks are still so red!"

I was pinned to the door, with Zaki just inches away from me. I felt my heartbeats right up to my ears, as incredible as it may sound.

"I'm really okay, Zaki." And I wasn't sure what came over me, but I circled my arms around him and laid my face in the center of his chest. He hugged me back, tighter. I had been embraced many times before, but it just felt different with him. We pulled away when we heard approaching footsteps.

"Bonjour, Zaki! Como sava?" Erdem, our French-Turkish colleague, just arrived from his overseas trip as well.

"Hi, Hanna! You look really flashy."

"Welcome back, Erdem."

I smiled at him and walked back to my desk and them in their respective offices. My chair offered relief. The tension inside me had not subsided. The feeling of his arms around me was still fresh. I closed my eyes and continued to bask in the afterglow of his embrace. A thought came to me. I withdrew my journal from the third layer of my side drawers. I wrote the following entry –

I will remember with fondness every touch, every hug, every kiss, every memory – no matter how trivial. I will always remember you.

Chapter 3

Thank heavens it's Thursday. The weekend would offer a respite to my tired body and weary mind. Though I couldn't hasten the hours, keeping myself busy would help me from getting agitated.

As I was going about my tasks, one of the sales managers approached me. He's upset over my supposed slow action to his request. I was trying to explain when he cut me off in a tone I found inappropriate. I expressed with tact my disapproval of his manner and tried shifting the focus back to his request. He became more hostile. When you correct a man, he would get angry. A heated argument ensued. After he left my desk, I was still reeling.

I phoned Roshie, our PRO, on her extension and told her that I would just be taking a walk outside for a few minutes. It was two in the afternoon and the sun was unforgiving. As I crossed the distance between our office and Park and Shop, I felt the kiss of the sun burning my cheeks. I went straight to the cold section where ice creams were kept. I grabbed myself a Magnum. I started on it the soonest as I stepped out of the store. On the way back to the office, I felt like my eyes were going to burst with tears. I nearly choked as I swallowed the ice cream in my mouth. I was trying not to cry. But tears were like rain, when it needed to fall, it would. I rushed to our pantry the moment I entered the office. I slumped on one of the dining chairs as my tears were flowing like water from a broken faucet. When I couldn't express my anger, crying helped me blow off the steam. I dropped the melting Magnum on my hand at the nearest bin. Standing for less than a minute was unbearable, given my weakening state. I pressed my back flat against the wall, and I felt my phone in my back pocket. I fished it out, and a thought came to me in an instant. Even before logic could kick in, I dialed Zaki's number. I was taken aback when I heard his voice.

"Hanna?" He inquired again.

"Can you come here, please? I need you." My voice was cracking in between sobs.

"Where are you?" Came his very worried response.

"In the pantry." I said weakly.

In minutes, the pantry door swung open, and I found myself in his arms. I was sobbing like a kid. He just let me cry for some time. There's a comforting energy enveloping me with each second I stay wrapped inside his arms. My adult mind was starting to protest this childish act. Yet my heart seemed perfectly at ease, reveling in the warmth of Zaki's comforting presence. One arm tightly wrapped around my waist, and the other gently holding my head, keeping me pressed against his chest. I inhaled his scent. He smelled divine. I felt divine being this close to him.

"Are you feeling okay now?" He asked when I moved my head to look up to him. I nodded. His eyes were beautiful. It had a way of making me forget everything, even for a moment.

"What happened, Hanna?"

I told him about the argument. Zaki was a man of intelligence and emotional maturity. Expectedly, his points on the matter were sensible. The gentleness with which he detailed my error by letting my temper get the better of me was like a child's medicine; it offered a cure but didn't taste bitter. He swatted my pride without hurting my ego.

I was quiet for some time. My mind heard and understood what he said. My heart, though, seemed to be rotating inside my ribcage, unable to stay put.

"I wish I could know what's on your mind now." He was looking down at me. I got self-conscious. All I managed to do was blink and smile shyly.

"Let's go back to work." He kissed my forehead and ushered me out of the pantry. Upon reaching my desk, he pulled my chair out and motioned me to sit. He pushed my hair back behind each ear and pinched my left cheek before walking back to his office. I was left numb and immobile, unable to function normally again for the remainder of the day. I felt lost inside, but I wasn't worried. I was confused, but I wasn't scared. *Zaki.*

I headed to the washroom and splashed water on my face. A thought was pressing itself into my consciousness, forcing me to acknowledge it. My heartbeat was going faster.

What's going on? You're in love. What? You're in love.

If I didn't know myself well enough I would be dead scared hearing my own mind this way.

*

At 15 minutes past six in the evening, my female colleagues were at my desk, all ready to leave for the day. I excused myself for a moment to bid goodbye to Zaki. When he saw me approaching, he stood from his desk with opened arms. No force was needed to make me walk into it, though I was hesitant to get as close. My heart seemed so conscious to feel the beating of his. But he drew me closer to him, aligning our torsos. I instinctively buried my face in the base of his neck, smelling his manliness. We stayed like that for a minute with neither of us moving. When I looked up to him, he smiled.

"Are you feeling better now?"

"Better than better." And I smiled back at him. He kissed me on the forehead and continued to hold me in his arms for a minute more. For the first time in a long time, I was so happy again. Every fiber of my body seemed to have been electrified. I felt so alive and grateful, too, for being so.

He positioned a chair close to his and asked me to sit down. Before doing so, I went back to our female colleagues and told them to go ahead. For hours, I forgot about the world below and outside. The office became our little paradise that night. We whiled away the time talking. Our conversation was moving seamlessly from one subject to the next. It felt refreshing being able to talk my mind out with little restraint. And he met my enthusiasm with his own vigor. When the topic moved to a lighter nature, he began teasing me. We started running and giggling while playing a silly tease and touch game. He became more physical toward me, always pulling me close to him when he caught me. He wouldn't let go unless I allowed him to kiss me! Each time his lips brushed my cheeks I warmed up. I felt currents running down straight to my heart, creating a glow in my eyes. Oh, how I wanted this to go on forever! A few minutes before ten o'clock, we were both panting and sweaty, having run around our office for hours. We were sitting on the floor, looking out and down at the ongoing traffic, when he asked me about my plan for the weekend. I hadn't been thinking right since that afternoon – or at least there was no coherence to my thoughts.

"Let's go for a swim at JBR."

"What time?" I couldn't hide the excitement in my voice. I loved the sea. Going to the beach was my most favorite pastime here in Dubai.

"After lunch perhaps, around three in the afternoon?" I agreed, playfully tapped him on the forehead, and made my attempt to run away. But he was quick to grab my foot and pulled me back down. I struggled, but he had a physical advantage, and so I ended up pinned to the ground, breathing heavily, and laughing. He slowly laid his head on my breasts. Panic rose to my throat all too suddenly. More than the physical encounter that could happen, there's something else, something deeper, that I feared. He felt the mad throbbing of my heart and raised his head to look at me.

"We better get going," I said and quickly sat up.

Earlier, I wished for this to never end. Now I was stepping on the brakes. He's staring at me with questioning eyes. I faked a smile and kissed his right cheek. My lips lingered a bit longer than they should have. He's not moving. The expression on his face hadn't changed; only his eyes seemed to be conveying a message my mind was too clouded to pick up right then.

"Zaki?" He didn't say anything and just pulled me closer to him. The kiss he planted on my forehead made its way to my heart. My internal system was shutting down, growing weak to his presence. A touch, a kiss, an embrace – these were what any woman would need. What I needed. But there was a difference if it was given out of genuine affection or just a fleeting attraction.

What are all these? What are we doing?

He motioned to stand and assisted me in doing the same. Once we were both standing, he leaned close and held me again, only this time tighter and more fervid. I felt his breath on my neck. Something passed between us, like an energy of some sort. I felt it. I slightly shuddered.

"Don't be afraid," his voice echoed all throughout my body, sending shockwaves that made my mind frantic.

"It's getting really late, Zaki. We must go home," I managed to sound firm by saying that. My heart detested my reasoning, but I couldn't afford to be careless.

"So, tomorrow at three?" His eyes were searching mine.

"Yes, sir!" I gave him a playful salute and a wink. He walked me to Lourdes' building, which was just three clusters away from our office. I was too exhausted to go home to DIP. He gave me a good-night hug before walking away toward the direction of Marina.

The lift had mirrors on all sides. I could see raw and varied emotions reflecting on my face, whichever side I turned. I felt boxed. I closed my eyes until I heard the ping of the elevator doors opening. I had been coming to Lourdes' place, and so my feet could walk to her unit without aid from my mind or eyes. I pressed on the doorbell. My eyes were still closed when she opened the door.

"What took you so long? I have been calling you," Lourdes sounded worried, and it wasn't good because she would hound me with questions.

"I'm sorry if I failed to answer. I was with Zaki." I went straight to her bathroom and started undressing myself. I was sweating down to my underwear. I couldn't recall meeting any man before him who had had that kind of effect on me. *Unbelievable*. I walked out naked and flopped to her bed, face down.

"Did you guys have sex?" Her tone was excited.

"No, babe," I muttered under my breath.

"Then why do you look so tired?"

"We were running around the office for hours." My lips curved into a smile, remembering our playfulness.

"Whatever." She never faked her annoyance.

"It's the truth. Why would I deny it if something did happen?"

"You smelled of him!" She hit my bottom with a pillow.

"It's because he kept hugging me whenever he caught me." I was laughing now, and I told her the rest of what happened.

"Be careful, babe. There are a lot of playful men here in Dubai." She warned me.

Could Zaki be one of them?

"Don't worry, babe. I'll not be easily taken in this time." The words came from my mind without conviction from my heart.

*

Close to three in the afternoon, Lourdes and I were both spread out on the sands in JBR. There were so many people today. The heat had teeth, though it was nothing compared to the emotion biting me hard deep inside. The vibration of my phone cut my reverie. It's a WhatsApp message from Zaki.

Zaki: Hi Hanna. I'm heading out to the beach now.
Me: Lourdes and I are already here. See you then.
Zaki: I'll be there in ten minutes. I'll call you.
Me: Okay

I was starting to get twisted inside again. I was in the middle of the crowd, and yet I felt isolated in my thoughts, getting lost in them even.

"Babe, where are you?" Lourdes sat up and looked at me.

"I feel scared, babe." I could be stoic with the world. My walls were down when I was with friends.

"What about exactly?"

"About what happened with me and Zaki yesterday. I was trying to understand why he behaved like that."

"Why do you need to understand it? What about last night that you find confusing? He likes you. Period. And it's obvious that you like him too. So just enjoy." She had a point. Perhaps I was overthinking again. My phone was vibrating once more. Zaki was calling.

"Hey. You are here?"

"Yes. Where are you at exactly?"

"I'm walking toward the blue, huge umbrella close to the changing tube. Can you see it? I'll meet you there."

My fogged brain made me forget to put on my dress. I only remembered it when it was too late for me to return for it. Zaki was beaming when he saw me. I felt somewhat too-exposed being in my bikinis. He leaned down and kissed me on the forehead. We walked closely back toward our spot. After a brief introduction with Lourdes, we went straight into the sea.

His male instinct seemed to be on full alert. He was evidently trying to send out a message to other guys that I wasn't available anymore. He was full on PDA. I loved being so close to Zaki. I loved the warmth that emanated from him. As it enwrapped me, I felt so protected and valued. I couldn't recall ever feeling that way, though I had been embraced many times in previous relationships. That's probably the reason why I was scared. I wasn't familiar with the feeling that he was arousing in me.

"You seem tense. What's wrong?" I had my arms around his neck, and his were wrapped around my waist.

"There are so many people here."

"So, what's the matter?"

"Our colleagues might see us, or your friends." I wasn't good at lying. My voice betrayed me every time.

"Are you really worried about that or me holding you like this?" That had finally caged me, in a manner of speaking. "What are you scared of, Hanna?" The concern in his voice was genuine.

"What are we doing, Zaki?" I wasn't sure it was right for me to ask that. But it had escaped my mouth faster than I could say Zaki's complete name, and for Arab men, it's at least four.

"Do I make you uncomfortable?"

"Not from the hug, but from the reason behind it. What are we doing? What is this?" Distress was noticeable in my voice now.

"Do you want to go back to shore and talk there instead?" I agreed. Being constantly buoyed by the waves was causing further dizziness in my heart.

We sat close to each other on my spread towel, and he covered me with his.

"I hope you're not angry at me." I felt a tug in my heart hearing him say that. I reached out to him and linked my right arm to his left.

"I'm not angry at you. I'm actually happy. I'm just scared because I don't understand what's happening."

"Love has no definition, Hanna. It doesn't require too much thinking, just acceptance. What do I need to explain to you?" His voice was gentle but firm. I felt his sincerity in it. In his eyes, I saw me. I started to tear up, for words had completely failed me at this moment. He wrapped his arm over my shoulder, and I buried my face in his neck while I sobbed quietly. Despite the hundreds of people there at the beach, with all the clamor around us, a certain stillness came over me. I felt the tides inside me starting to calm down.

"Hanna?" He checked on me after being quiet for some time.

"Hmm?"

He raised my chin and angled my face directly to his. I smiled at him. He smiled back. I kissed his jaw. His stubble tickled my lips. It's so easy to get lost in Zaki. If love was a destination, then the heart would know when one had finally arrived. I thought then that I had. I was home. After years of wandering about, though I wasn't entirely lost, it felt amazing to finally find my place. Being this close to him, feeling his body next to me seems so natural. His right hand caressing mine, tracing the outline of nerves visible because of my

Chinese fair skin, walking his fingers on my knuckles. It felt so good. I couldn't recall a similar instance I felt the same when my former boyfriends held my hand. I looked up at him, and his eyes were smiling at me. So simple a gesture but had a profound impact.

"Do you want to go back down into the water?"

I looked at the sea and the sea of people in it.

"I think it's perfect where we are."

"If you say so, mademoiselle." And he winked at me.

"I wonder where Lourdes is." For some time, she had completely slipped out of my mind. I searched amongst the crowd.

"Does she know how to swim?"

"Yes, and a confident one, too."

"Then nothing to worry about. She's just out there somewhere."

And just then I saw her emerged from the water, looking worn out. She lied down straight on her spread towel upon coming back.

"Did you have a good swim?" I asked as she drew in air through her mouth.

"That's a big crowd. I had to be somewhere deep so I could swim well."

Indeed, it's a huge crowd today. Lourdes and I were here every weekend. We had breakfast by the sands at seven in the morning and would be home after dinner, close to eight in the evening. We knew by face the regular beachgoers – families with children, couples, and group of friends who enjoy lounging by the shore and under the sun like we do. Today it's a party with all sorts of activities happening simultaneously. There's a happy, good vibe in the air. And inside, I felt the glow from the flame of love that was just starting to grow. I felt my cheeks heating up.

"What are you thinking about just now?" Zaki asked, looking at me. There were a thousand stacks of thoughts in my mind, but why spoil the moment with words? I responded with a smile and reached for his hand. It's big enough to cover mine almost entirely. Our fingers instinctively curled around each other, and he gave my hand a gentle squeeze. A mundane act that became special simply because it was him.

After a sumptuous early dinner, he walked me and Lourdes back to her apartment building. We exchanged kisses on both cheeks and a half-minute embrace. Then he released me only to pull me again for a quick kiss on the forehead. I giggled and looked up to him smiling.

"Good night to you both."

"Good night, Zaki."

In the elevator on the way up to her floor, Lourdes' remark reddened my cheeks.

"You look in love, girl."

"I am, yes."

"He's a Muslim, right?" I didn't see where she was getting at here, but I gave a nod of affirmation.

"That's okay with you? You don't see an issue with his religion?" It completely threw me off course. Zaki's religion had never been a matter I paid any thought to since day one. I remained quiet until we reached her apartment. I wasn't certain how to respond.

"I'm not trying to spoil your fun. All I'm saying is that his religion might post a concern for you both later down the road." I kept quiet and turned my back on her so she could untie my bikini top.

"Hanna?" She pressed on me.

"I'm listening, babe. I'm processing your words." *And I'm having a hard time doing so at the moment.* "Can I shower first?" I didn't wait for her to answer. I stepped into the tub and pulled back the shower curtain. I stayed under the shower for some minutes, hoping to wash off Lourdes' words that seemed to be slowly seeping through my pores.

In my journal that night, I wrote down what I couldn't dare ask anyone openly.

Why does it matter?
Love knows no religion, but in itself can be one.
Love is taught in every faith, across the globe.
Why should differing religions matter between two people in love?

For the next few days, this thought followed me everywhere. It's like a shadow behind my more pressing thoughts. It would come uninvited and would just stop me from whatever I was doing. I had to really talk myself out of my own thoughts. And it didn't help that Zaki had been in and out of the office, traveling from one country to the next for meetings and assisting his team on their operations at our customers' refineries. I saw him only one day each in two successive weeks. Every day that he was away, my heart was painfully aware of the distance that separated us.

*

Saturday mornings were my H and M (Hanna and Molly) time.

Molly: What exactly is it that's troubling you?
Me: A friend of mine here brought up Zaki's religion once. I hadn't been settled since.
Molly: Why? Did she say something critical of Zaki's beliefs?
Me: She just said that it might create some issues for us Later on.
Molly: I know that Muslims are allowed to have a Relationship with Christians and Jews. They can marry outside of their faith. Have you asked her to explain what she meant by what she said?
Me: No, I didn't because I didn't want to dwell on the matter. But it has disturbed my mind ever since.
Molly: You always overthink everything, Hanna. Relax. There is nothing to be confused about love. There is nothing to be scared about it either. Love is an experience. Enjoy and live it!

I wasn't confused. I wasn't scared. Zaki was a good man, the best I had met so far. But I had to admit that Lourdes' words kind of cast on him a different shade, for which it's difficult for me to understand then or determine why.

But Molly was right. Love, indeed, was an experience, and I never had it in the way I was experiencing it with Zaki. Something inside me was telling me that I could trust my feelings for him. If I never mind his religion at the beginning was probably because there was no reason for it. And if, indeed, our religions could be a cause for concern for either of us, how come, Zaki had never displayed any such worries? I refused to believe that he was just playing it well.

I closed my eyes as a way to calm my mind. Without any thought, I looked up at the sky. It's a clear day, with hardly any clouds on the horizon.

Don't ask for the rain, Hanna. Calm down. Breathe and just love.

Chapter 4

2015

"I'm going home for Eid. Come with me."

I had always been fascinated by the pyramids in Egypt. I was seven years old when I first saw pictures of it in one of the books our father brought home from his travels abroad. Through the years, my interest to learn and understand the deep and rich history of Egypt never waned. Research studies and reports in our geography and history classes further fostered my obsession with the country and its earliest people. Even outside the scope of our classroom discussions I read about Egypt, postponing my trip home a bit later, especially on Fridays. I remember sitting down on the floor at the corner of the history section in our library, leaning against the shelf and cradling a big book on my lap, the vivid illustrations in it of ancient Egypt drawing me in completely. Then, while on the school bus on the way home, to help me bear the traffic, I imagined myself walking around the temple in Karnak, wearing a pharaoh's crown. I particularly liked the one with an upright cobra and a vulture on it. I found it autocratic and bold, arrogant even, but that only added appeal to it.

"Hanna, do you want to come to Egypt with me?" The first time he brushed it up to me, I was in the middle of answering an email. His words registered in my mind, but I couldn't respond to him just then.

"Of course, I would go with you." I stood from my chair and gave him a kiss on one cheek. We always embraced after, and we didn't pull away immediately, except if we heard anyone of our colleagues approaching. His arms were my most favorite place in the world. "I'll coordinate with our travel agency for my visa."

"Good. I'll go ahead of you for a few days. I'll spend some time with my family. Maybe it would be good if you go to Alexandria first. There are good tourist spots to see there. Then take the train heading to Cairo a day after, but get off at Tanta. I'll come and get you at the station."

"It sounds good to me."

"There's a cheap but nice hotel within walking distance to the sea in Alexandria. I'll give you the details of it later." I was hanging on to his every word as the excitement was building up inside me, brick after brick.

Egypt. My childhood dream was coming true. And I was going to see it with a very special man! My happiness was overwhelming me, causing my eyes to water. As a child, I had dreamed a million and one dreams and fantasies. Life had a way of dissolving our desires to continue on dreaming some of those dreams once adulthood sets in. It would take a courageous, determined heart to stay true to those aspirations and see about their fulfillment. I felt a sense of pride, thinking I was about to accomplish an important dream I held dear in my heart. With a man like Zaki by my side, it would easily be the trip of a lifetime.

The visa seal on my passport solidified my trip. I had no doubt that I would get an approval. My mind was actually surprised at my confidence, but I didn't question the source of it. Lately, I realized the more I thought of things the more I got confused. I didn't want to be the antithesis of my own happiness. I closed my eyes, as had been my customary gesture when I wanted to stop myself from thinking. Just then, the image of the grand pyramids in Giza flashed on the screen in my mind. I imagined myself on a horse, traversing the distance between the pyramids and stopping by in front of each to marvel at its beauty. The vibration of my phone brought me back to Dubai. It's a WhatsApp message from Zaki.

Zaki: Hanna, what's the update on your visa?

I took a picture of my visa and sent it to him and captioned it with an emoji with heart-shaped eyes. He sent a wide grinning emoji and a thumbs-up to express how pleased he was with the decision.

It's still two weeks before my flight. Zaki was still in France for a series of meetings, but every day he helped me prepare for the trip through our communication on WhatsApp. One weekend I went to shop for some blouses with long sleeves to be worn on the trip. Zaki told me to choose light fabrics so I wouldn't be discomforted by the heat, though I would still be properly covered.

Zaki: And Hanna, leave your bikinis in Dubai!

My response was a frowning emoji. Apart from seeing the historical sites in some countries I dreamed of visiting, I also wanted to swim in their seas. No two beaches were the same, though they may have looked like so. I could tell the differences between each of the beaches I visited all these years.

> **Zaki:** You're going to Egypt, Hanna. We're still a Conservative Muslim country. Hotels and private resorts allow their guests to be in swimming attires within their premises. You'll be staying in my apartment in Cairo. Your only access to the sea would be through the public beach. Nothing skimpy is allowed in public.

> I acknowledged his admonitions with a winking emoji.

> **Zaki:** I'm serious, Hanna. Egypt, in reality, may not be the same as how you read about it.

Our conversation closed after I gave him my word that I would do as he asked. I crossed out "bikinis" on my list of must-bring. A part of me was slightly sad, thinking I wouldn't be able to enjoy the beach in Egypt on this first trip. I consoled myself with another thought that I would have some space in my luggage for some souvenirs. I looked at my bookshelf and imagined a pyramid statue and maybe a bust of Hatshepsut or Nefertari on its shelves as bookends. It was enough to get me more excited.

*

A day before Eid Al-Fitr, I took an early morning flight to Alexandria. The 4-hour journey went by smoothly. I usually fell asleep once the plane took off, regardless of how short the trip may be. It's not the case today. My excitement was growing each minute, mile after mile, as we got closer to our destination. 15 minutes before we landed, the captain's voice could be heard across the plane. He invited us to take a peek at the scenery below. The landscapes could not be compared to Dubai. Hardly were there skyscrapers in Alexandria, but my excitement, nevertheless, was very high.

After the smooth landing and the quick screening at Immigration, I went straight to the arrival section to search for my service sent by the hotel. My driver was a clean-shaven middle-aged man. He said his name was Ibrahim. He spoke good English and was a very good road companion. I didn't notice the almost hour-long travel from the airport to the hotel because I got absorbed in his stories.

The hotel was simple, with castle-like interiors. After a quick chat with the friendly staff at the front desk, I was directed toward the elevators. My room was sleek and fronting what looked like a flea market located at the back of the hotel. I decided to lie down for a while and take in the fact that I was in Egypt. I was close to falling asleep when I heard a sound inside my bag. I fished my iPhone out. It's a WhatsApp message from Zaki asking for confirmation of my arrival. I sent him a quick selfie by the window. He said he would see me tomorrow evening in Tanta. I went back to bed to nap.

The afternoon call for prayer at 3:30 woke me up. I slept a solid three hours. I stepped out of my clothes and had a shower. Then I went down and asked for a map of the city with the tourist spots highlighted so I could roam around. The doorman hailed me a taxi and instructed the driver in Arabic to take me anywhere I wished to go and to bring me back there afterward. I surmised that as he was pointing to the map in my hand. The driver agreed, and we went on our way. The driver couldn't speak a single English word, and neither could I in Arabic – except Shukran – Thank you. Weeks leading up to this trip, Zaki was out on business meetings abroad, and I was busy with my duties in the office. It crossed my mind to learn basic Arabic, but I never got around to doing so. So the driver and I communicated through sign language, meaning I pointed at a destination on the map and we drove there. When I wanted my pictures taken, I would hand him my phone. To angle my photos correctly, he directed me to move either to the left or right and motioned for me to tilt my head or my entire body to either side.

He took me from the Montaza Palace, with a nice view of the beach, to the Citadel of Qaitbay. I enjoyed walking about in that great old fortress, especially inside the hallway. There were obvious renovations done to it, but the old grandeur of the place was still there. I took my time discovering every section of the citadel and peeking through each square hole where the canyons were once placed. I had a few photos taken at the very top and had the main tower as my background. It's a workout to cover the entire area. I lingered at the top to look out at the coast. There were fishing boats docked close to the shore. The streets below were busy and filled with people enjoying the sea breeze and the small shops nearby.

We stopped by on the seaside before returning to the hotel. Alexandria was getting dark, and the horizons were decorated with beautiful colors that only nature could mix so well. The Mediterranean Sea was glistening with a soft glow from the fading sun. I took a snapshot and sent it to Zaki. Then I spent a few minutes in silence, taking in the view.

Alexandria today was far from its glory days in the past. I looked about in my surrounding, imagining what this city was like then. Opulence must be everywhere instead of the garbage that now littered the streets, uncollected and unmind. Well-groomed men and ladies walked about with pride and confidence, knowing they were the center of the world. My driver waved at me and asked if I was okay with a gesture of thumbs up. I must have looked weary while I was going through my daydream of the past, and it alarmed him. I answered by raising my right thumb in affirmation. I looked at the sea again and stayed until the sun disappeared from sight.

*

I was just finishing my light dinner in the room when the phone by the bedside table rang. I picked it up and a friendly voice greeted me on the other end. He introduced himself as Eslam, the one who assisted me on my reservation. I recalled his friendliness on the telephone. However, I paid not much thought to it so I was quite surprised by his call. He asked if I wanted to see the city at night. It's a tempting offer, but I imagined how furious Zaki would be to find out about it tomorrow. I thanked him for the proposition and reasoned that I was tired and would rather sleep early.

*

A dreamless night passed, and the call for morning prayer woke me up. I checked my phone for the time. It's just 16 minutes past the hour of five. I hadn't slept long. I set the alarm on my phone at eight and willed myself to fall back to sleep despite my awakening enthusiasm to start my day early to see the rest of Alexandria.

A little past nine, while having breakfast, my phone vibrated. It's a WhatsApp message from a local number. I thumbed open my phone to check who it was from. It's the same guy from the reservations team. I accepted his invitation, thinking it would be safe to go with him in broad daylight.

We agreed to meet at Pompey's Pillar. I got there earlier. The Bibliotheca of Alexandria was closed because it was a holiday, so I went straight to Pompey's. The ancient site hadn't been opened yet. It was summer, and early in the day, the sun was very hot. I decided to seek shelter in a shop that sold mobile phones across the street. The kids started to crowd around me, curious and eager. A cute little girl with thick curls smiled at me shyly. I smiled back. They erupted in giggles, which amused me. They're talking to me in Arabic.

"I can't speak Arabic."

Then a woman with a baby on her hip and deep brown eyes with very long eyelashes came forward and greeted me. She said the kids were remarking about my dimples. It made me smile again. The woman spoke some English and asked me if I was from China and why I was there. I told her I was from the Philippines. She said she had never seen a Filipino before. Zaki told me once that he had no knowledge whether there were people from my country who had ever worked in Egypt. So the woman's comment didn't surprise me.

The men in the shop joined in on our conversation. One of them asked me if I was engaged, pointing to the gold ring on my right hand. I responded, "No." Apparently, in Egypt, when a woman is seen wearing a ring on her right ring finger it means that she was engaged. Then the ring would move to the left ring finger upon marriage. After learning that I was single, what one of the guys asked me next made me laugh so hard.

"So I can marry you?" He went on to detail his work and his ability to support me. I was restraining myself from laughing harder. Zaki told me to be careful while going about here in Alexandria. He said some men might approach me, but I should just ignore them and move along. What he didn't brief me on was the persistence of these men and their reluctance to accept rejection. Two more men chimed in and were presenting themselves to me. The brown-eyed woman and I just kept laughing. One guard from Pompey's Pillars cut through our merriment and said I could then come in.

The site was surprisingly small but quite deep. Some sections were cordoned off because of the ongoing excavation. According to many archaeologists who had done excavation work in Egypt and those still ongoing, much of the country's history was still submerged in the sands. How deep they would still have to dig was something they could never be certain of.

I took pictures of every stone with carvings on it, columns, the small version of the Sphinx similar to that in Giza, and artifacts scattered about in the site. I posted it all on my Facebook account in real time. It's my way of keeping my family abreast of my time here and sharing with my friends the adventure I was on. I was the lone visitor at that hour, so I covered the whole site in a short time. There's a shaded area where visitors could lounge and rest after the tour. It's elevated to some levels, so one could have a good look at the entire site. I opted to sit there while waiting for Eslam. I looked out at the surrounding area. The site of Pompey's Pillars was in the middle of what seemed like a busy neighborhood. There were houses and low-rise buildings all around it. It made me wonder how they felt being in a place where much had happened back in their history. Alexandria was the first capital of Egypt, leading to modern times. The city was named after Alexander the Great and was an important complex during his reign. It must have been an exciting time.

A lanky guy in a green shirt who looked seemingly young entered the gate, pressing the pause button in my head. He was looking in my direction. I knew right away that it was Eslam. While he was walking toward me, I silently tried guessing his age. Not that I was interested in him in any way. The voice on the phone was deep and sounded very manly. His appearance, though, didn't show any of that. Up close, he was very attractive, with mesmerizing amber eyes.

"Hi. I'm Eslam." I received his right hand and introduced myself. "Sorry if I made you wait. A lot of people are out these days because of the holiday," his voice sounded different in person, slightly unsettling me.

"It's alright. I noticed that too on the way to the Bibliotheca earlier and on my way here."

"You were already at the Bibliotheca? Alone?" His tone had a hint of panic in it.

"Yes, but it's closed. So I came straight here instead."

"You've been alone all this time?"

I couldn't understand why it was becoming a matter of concern for him.

"Yes."

"Wow! You're a brave girl." His smile could make a younger girl blush easily. He sure was really charming. "So, shall we take a look around?"

"I already have."

"Oh. Pictures perhaps?"

"I'm done with that as well." And I smiled at him. He was looking embarrassed. "Hey, it's alright. Perhaps we can go elsewhere."

He suggested we head to the Roman amphitheater in Kom El Dekka. I had no idea where that was or how far we were from it. But I agreed, thinking what an experience it would be to see the ancient remains of the Roman conquest in this more ancient city.

Once outside, I tried hailing a taxi, but he said it would be cheaper to take public transportation. I silently detested the idea, but I thought I would try it even for once. He hailed the approaching van. There's no signage on it, so I wondered how he knew where it was heading. When the door opened, the passengers were looking at me, curious and baffled. I ignored their stares and went to the very back of the van. Eslam sat beside me. I asked how much the fare was. He ignored me and handed coins to the ones sitting in front of us. I learned that Egyptian men would not let a lady pay for anything if it could be helped. Millions of girls would be delighted at this fact, though I found it belittling me in a way. Minutes after, he said something in Arabic, and the van stopped.

"Come on, we're getting down." That was quick. My mind had not been able to embrace the whole idea of Egyptian masculinity yet.

"You're cute," he said upon getting down.

"Excuse me?"

"When you're thinking, you're cute." He lightly pinched my left cheek while smiling. My blood rushed upward, heating up my cheeks.

"How did you know I'm thinking?"

"Your eyes, focused and unblinking, and your lips were twitching." Wow! What keen eyes he had.

"Interesting," it's all I could think of saying. *Has he been observing me all along? Has he noticed how uncomfortable I am having him around me?*

"You're thinking again. I wish you could tell me what's on your mind." Smart, charming, and observant, he's shaping out to be Mr. Wonder Boy by the minute!

"Nothing important, just random thoughts." *Like how cute you are!* I looked up to him and smiled.

A short walk and we reached the old theater. While we were buying our tickets, two guards approached us. They spoke to Eslam. I didn't understand what they were discussing about but I knew it was me. They kept looking at me. After some minutes, we walked off and started the tour of the place. I asked Eslam about the held up at the gate. He said the guards were asking what our relationship was with each other. He went on to explain that he informed them that I was a tourist at the hotel where he was working and that he was showing me around. Silently, I was scolding myself for not learning Arabic beforehand.

The ruins of the Roman amphitheater were beautiful, though relatively small in my opinion. I guessed it's because in the books they made it look substantially larger and the area more vast. Some of the columns were still there, but not as imposing as I had imagined. The benches that looked similar to stairs, where people must have sat back then, had been excavated to some depth – 13 levels so far. I couldn't tell, though, how deep it still had to go since the digging on many parts of the site seemed to have just started. An area right in front of the theater had been excavated, and wooden planks were placed on top of it to bridge the gap the open ground had created. This way, visitors could reach the theater and have their pictures taken there.

We walked some more and into the innermost parts. It would have been easy to get lost in this place. There were square-shaped quarters and narrow walkways. I thought they were perhaps the cells where the gladiators were imprisoned. The Romans were well known for their fondness for such kind of entertainment.

"This place also had a bath house. Those quarters may have been the changing rooms," Eslam said when I remarked at how odd it was to find a bathtub there.

"What is a bathhouse?" The picture in my mind was that of a sauna or steam room in today's time.

He opened his mobile phone and showed me images on Google of Greek men lounging in a huge pool wearing only what seemed like loincloth.

"Alexandria was one of Alexander's most favorite cities. Of course, there's got to be bathhouses here. After all, this amphitheater had varied uses before. When the Romans built this, they used this for artistic purposes, where music and poetry were publicly shared with those gathered here.

"In the time of the Byzantine Empire, this place served as a venue where the public gathered to discuss about politics and other concerns.

"It's only during the time when Islam was introduced here that this place was ignored, probably because they didn't know what to use it for since it didn't resemble in any way to the structures of our mosques. And then nature took over and buried it in the sands." I hinted at something in his voice, an emotion I couldn't identify. I leaned against the wall of one open chamber. I wanted to understand the sentiment in his tone.

"If given the chance, would you choose to have lived then than now?" Zaki and another colleague seemed to have little desire to talk about their ancient past. Surely, they had been taught about their history at schools. But Eslam's obvious passion for his country's history had an underlying, strong emotion attached to it.

"We're going downhill, Hanna. There's unrest everywhere in the country. Our economy is in very bad shape. So yes, I would have loved to have lived in the past, in the times of the great pharaohs, where there were progression and order. I don't understand all that is happening now." His words made me quiet for a while. My heart felt the sadness of his. I may have had a good understanding of what was happening in their country, and in the region as a whole, but I opted not to press on. Not every 20-something could understand the maddening concepts of politics. I rubbed his shoulder lightly instead.

"Shall we continue with the tour?"

Another section at the far end was closed off with a notice advising visitors of the danger of the ongoing excavation. It looked like stairs to me, as the excavated rocks seemed to be winding down. He had the same impression.

"I think those were stairs, and they led down to the common bath area, where men continued on their conversations that might have started from the theater."

I nodded at him. I was meaning to ask him something else, but when I chanced upon the time on my watch, I was reminded of Zaki. I told Eslam I needed to be back at the hotel to check out and then head to the train station to go to Tanta. He insisted that we drop by their house for lunch. He said his mom was eager to meet me.

"I told her I was going to meet you. She asked me to bring you home to celebrate with us."

I wasn't expecting to meet anyone on this trip, more so go to anyone's house to celebrate. I didn't know if it was offensive to refuse such an invitation, especially since Eid was like Christmas to Muslims. I reluctantly agreed, but I told Eslam that I must get to Tanta before dark.

On the way, he suggested perhaps I wanted to see the museum. I instantly affirmed. So far, all I had seen were rocks used for various purposes, such as very old structures, and artifacts, among others. The ancient Egyptians had quarried millions of rocks during their time. But that wasn't the only thing they were famous for. When the name Egypt was mentioned, the first thing that came to people's minds, apart from the famous pyramids, were the mummies. I definitely wanted to see some. The museum would be where they could be found now.

We rode in a public van again. A few minutes into our journey, he signaled to the driver that we were getting off. A short walk after and we were in front of the Alexandria National Museum. On the outside, it looked like a mansion, an imposing all-white beauty. Inside, priceless collections delighted my eyes and excited my mind, so much so that I became oblivious to time.

Amazing pieces of jewelry from the start of the Islamic era, Roman busts of important people, statues and beautifully decorated vases, items recovered during the time of the Coptic Christians, Greek figurines of sophisticated women, animal heads carved on granite stones, and other valuable artifacts that archaeologists found during excavation campaigns were all on display. Some of the earliest mummies they had unearthed were in the basement. I was beyond thrilled when my eyes laid on the mummy at the center display. It's fully intact. Its sarcophagus had intricate drawings and details on it. The original colors with which it was painted were still very visible, though some parts were damaged. I allowed the genius of the ancient Egyptians to put me in a trance. I was lost for words. I had seen hundreds of pictures of mummies in books and in documentaries I had watched. Even then, I had been deeply intrigued. Now, standing in front of this wonder, I was in awe, so much so that I didn't realize I had been quiet the entire time we were there. I felt his hand on my back. The contact pulled me back to the present.

"Hanna?"

"I'm alright. I'm just very happy." There may be people who were appalled at the mere sight of a coffin, more so of a dead body. But what was lying before me then was a masterpiece of its own kind. My eyes gave way to tears. I felt humbled and privileged at the same time. This dead person had lived before me lifetimes ago. His remains had survived the ravages of time to come to us now – to me – and to fill me with an exquisite delight that came second only to love.

"I would love to hear your mind at this minute." Eslam was carefully treading around my open emotion.

"At the moment, there are no words good enough for me to express what I'm really feeling." I wasn't being dismissive. The beauty of this ancient wonder could really render anyone speechless.

I moved on to the other mummies on display and committed to memory how each one looked like. Cameras weren't allowed inside the museum. Eslam was patient enough to be two steps behind me all the time, probably worried that I might faint any minute due to so much excitement.

I was probably on my third go around the mummies when he thought it might become more difficult to pull me away from there if we stayed a minute longer, so Eslam reminded me of the time. I didn't want to pay extra for checking out late, so I managed to get my feet moving in the direction of the exit door.

My luggage had been ready since that morning before I left, so it didn't take me long to vacate the room. The friendly guy at the front desk who assisted me when I arrived yesterday was the same one on duty today. I thanked him promptly, then I took my leave. Eslam was waiting for me at the corner of the street. Hotel staff were not allowed to go out with guests, so we were not to be seen together.

A short taxi ride and we reached their place. He lived in a modest community in Alexandria. Their house was on the fourth floor of an apartment complex. I felt the burn on my derriere upon reaching their floor. His mom opened the door. She was probably in her late forties. She's beautiful. She enveloped me in her arms the moment I stepped in. I felt the warmth of her personality in that brief contact. I was pleased but also worried that I might not reach Tanta early.

I sent a quick WhatsApp message to Zaki when I was left to myself in their living room. He must have been anticipating my message. His response was immediate and with a hint of sarcasm.

Zaki: I forgot to tell you to leave your charms in Dubai.

His message made me smile, though. I was about to put the phone back into my bag when it vibrated again. It's another message from him.

Zaki: I forgot to brief you on Egyptian foods. Try to get a little of everything you will be offered so as not to offend your hosts.

I slightly panicked at the thought that I might be offered something spicy and be forced to swallow it or risk offending the host party. I thought of asking Zaki, but then Eslam walked in. Though I was feeling highly awkward, I raised the question to him instead.

"Don't worry, Hanna. We don't like spicy food too. My mom rarely cooks any spicy dishes, except when my uncle comes for a visit." I sighed in relief. He was introducing me to the people in the pictures hanging in frames on the walls when his mom walked in.

"Your uncle's on his way, actually," and she grinned. Eslam and I exchanged glances.

"Don't worry, dear, I will not serve you anything spicy." I smiled shyly with burning cheeks. I didn't realize she heard us, given all the noises in the kitchen. She brushed my crimson cheek lightly with the back of her right hand and said perhaps we could swim while she was preparing the food.

"Swim where?" I couldn't hide the excitement in my voice.

"There's a public beach not far from here."

"But I have been told that I can't wear a bikini on the public beach."

"You can, but we will have to be some distance away from the others." Panic returned to me and slowly rose to my throat when Eslam winked at me. I imagined Zaki's face with eyes narrowing from annoyance because of this presumptuous idea.

"I don't have a bikini," I said flatly, hoping to discourage him.

"We can go to the mall while Mom cooks. This way, you can see more of the city too," he sounded eager.

"How old are you, Eslam?"

"Why?"

"I'm just curious."

"24." I was right about my assumptions earlier. Now I understood the excitement in his tone. It's the age of raging hormones. How best to deal with this situation?

"Ready?" I was absorbed in my thoughts. He had to nudge me. "Hanna?"

"I don't think I want to swim, Eslam. But I do want to take a walk and see the city more."

"Okay then, let's go."

We bid his mom goodbye and went down from their apartment floor, which in itself was like a warm-up already. I reminded myself of the ordeal later, when we came back. Outside, some of their neighbors were gathered on the streets and were greeting each other. Eslam approached an old man. They shook hands and exchanged kisses on both cheeks. Eslam introduced me to him. The man took my hand and held it to his chest. The gesture baffled me.

"It's about time, Eslam." Saleem smiled, displaying tobacco-stained teeth. He was addressing Eslam but his gaze was fixed on me. I felt unsettled, but I opted not to say anything. I gave him a curt smile and looked away, gently pulling my hand.

This has to end now.

I could hold my bearing in any uncomfortable situation, but my cheeks would always betray me. I pretended to be looking around their street, just so I could hide the redness of my face.

"You're so quiet," he broke the silence minutes after we turned at the corner of their street.

"I have nothing to say." *Nothing that your young, excited mind can comprehend.* I may never see him again, so I might as well play along. After all, what harm could this do? I checked my watch again. It's almost one in the afternoon. I was making a mental calculation as to what time I must leave in order to get to Tanta before dark.

"You have been checking your watch. I find it impolite. It's like you can't wait to be parted from me."

My ears reddened with irritation at his words. I held my tongue behind my teeth for as long as I could. This was immaturity talking, and I didn't want to go down to that level.

"I need to get to Tanta by dinner time," I said in a matter-of-fact tone.

"Are you meeting someone there?" He was standing in front of me, his amber eyes searching mine.

"Yes, I am," I said dryly but with full earnestness.

"Who?" His tone was a bit aggressive.

"Watch your tone." My mood was beginning to get darker so quickly.

"I really like you, Hanna. I'm sorry. I guess I'm just jealous."

Really now?!

Under the heat of the Egyptian sun, on a street I didn't know the name of, and with all these people looking at us as they passed, I was having the most incredulous conversation with someone I barely knew. Unbelievable! My temper was threatening to overflow.

Calm yourself, Hanna. Breathe.

"Eslam, I think it's best we go back to your house so I can get my things. I should really get going," my voice belied my simmering anger.

"Look, I'm sorry, Hanna. It's just that I really like…"

"You don't even know me." I snapped at him. I saw the shock on his face. I was aware that men in this region were not accustomed to having women talk back to them. But I wasn't from this region, and I would speak when crossed. I turned to the direction from where we came and started walking.

"Hanna, wait, please." Eslam grasped my right elbow.

"Eslam, I'm flattered by your admiration. But I'm older than you are, and I'm in love with someone else. He's waiting for me in Tanta." I tore my eyes from his face and resumed walking.

"Is he an Egyptian too?" I ignored his question and continued at my pace. "Hanna?"

"What is it to you?" My irritation was mounting with his intrusiveness and with my foolishness in accepting his invitation. I would have been well on my way had I refused.

"Hanna, I'm sorry. Please don't be angry. Please." My heart heard the tenderness in his voice. I turned to him and clasped his hands in mine.

"Eslam, you're a really cute guy and very smart. I enjoyed my time with you this morning. I appreciate you coming over to show me around. But please understand that we can never be. I love someone else." I turned from him again, and this time I was determined not to look back or stop.

"Hanna. Hanna." I kept on walking. He grabbed my hand, but I pulled it away. He stepped in front of me and politely asked me to stop.

"It's Eid. Please don't break my heart." There was raw pain in his eyes. I studied his face while I willed my mind to word my response properly.

"When we're hurting because we can't have the one we want, it's easy to put the blame on that person without realizing that it's us who bring it up on ourselves." I made a full stop. I kept my eyes on his face, reading the impact of my words beginning to moist his eyes. *Ah, the fragility of youth.* I must salvage his pride though, or whatever was left of his self-esteem.

"If the situation had been different, I'm sure I would choose to be with someone like you." I pulled him into an embrace and let go seconds after. "Please, let's go back to the house."

We walked back in uncomfortable silence. I would rather have it than hear any more from him. When we reached their apartment complex, he asked me to go up ahead of him. I did just that without asking why and kept climbing the stairs almost without pause. My heart was pounding when I reached their door. I tried catching my breath first before knocking. A pretty girl, probably about 15 years old, with eyes a similar color to Eslam opened the door.

"Hanna! They're back!" I was hesitant to come in. I wanted to leave but looked like I would be delayed.

"Oh, what a lovely girl you are, my dear!" said the woman, whom I nearly mistook for Eslam's mom the moment I entered. She pulled me into an embrace after the customary kisses on both cheeks. "Where is Eslam?"

"He's talking to a friend downstairs." *Imaginary one, though.*

"Okay. I'm Najima, Eslam's aunt. His mom is my older sister." Now I understood the striking similarities. "This is my husband, Abdullah." I extended my hand in recognition.

"And I'm Naseema." The pretty girl volunteered her identity. I shook her hand and made a positive remark about her beautiful amber eyes. The door creaked open, and Eslam walked in. The sadness was still evident on his face, but he seemed pacified. Naseema rushed to him and he lifted her for a hug. Afterward, he greeted Naseema's parents while the girl was still playfully clinging to his neck. I excused myself and went to his bedroom, where he had left my luggage earlier.

"You're leaving?" I was startled by the rise in pitch of Naseema's voice upon stepping back out to their living area. They all looked at me. I felt the blood rush to my face.

"I need to get to Tanta before dark." I tried not to sound harsh so as not to twist the knife in Eslam's heart, so to speak. But sometimes, regardless of what we do or don't do, we still end up hurting some people. I guessed I would just have to live with that. Moments after he left for the dining room, his mom came out from the kitchen, wiping her hands on her apron.

"Hanna, dear, why are you leaving so early?" The tenderness in her voice threatened to weaken my resolve.

"There's someone waiting for me in Tanta. We agreed to meet by dinner." Silence. It seemed like the whole house was put on pause – no movements, no sound, nothing. I didn't realize how long a minute could be until then. "I wish I could stay a bit longer, but tonight had already been planned beforehand. I'm really sorry." I walked toward her and reached for her hand. The warmth of her personality could still be felt from her damped, cold hands as she took mine in both of hers.

"No worries, my dear. We will eat now. Eslam, prepare the table," she called out behind her. "It's a long journey. You'll be hungry, so better eat first."

"It's done, Ma." Eslam emerged from the dining room with a pained look on his face. I knew too well how to soothe such an ache away. But doing so now would only do much worse than good. I looked away.

I sat on the single sofa by the door of their balcony so as not to be seated next to Eslam, thinking that he might take the opportunity to press himself on me again since everyone else was in the kitchen. I fished my phone from my bag. There's a message from Zaki.

Zaki: Are you at the train station now?

I wanted to go for the truth, but it's difficult to explain the whole context of my situation through a WhatsApp message.

Me: I have been invited to a simple family feast. I'll be Heading to the station after here.
Zaki: You mean to tell me you are at a stranger's house? Where did you meet him?

I wondered how he could have guessed the gender of my new friend. But I guessed it was something innate about Egyptians, for just then Eslam's voice interrupted my thought processing.

"He's probably asking where you are." I looked at him, and his eyes were burning with both jealousy and sadness.

"Yes." And I looked back at the phone in my hand but unable to continue typing my response for Zaki. Eslam's emotions were like a rushing flood smashing against the gates of my heart, insisting to fill me with it.

"I wish I was him," he said it in an almost inaudible voice, yet my ears heard it. I felt a tug in my heart.

"Come, Hanna, come sit here, and we will eat now." His mother's invitation was a welcome intrusion into my thoughts. I was walking toward the dining table when I remembered Zaki. I must send a reply.

Me: The guy works at the hotel where I stayed. He

introduced me to his family. I'll leave after the meal. I couldn't decline. They're such sweet people.

I put my phone back in my bag and was walking toward the table when I heard it vibrate against the other contents inside. I chose to ignore it.

The sooner I get this over with, the sooner I'm out of here.

But I immediately felt a pang of guilt with this thought. I was a stranger welcomed into this warm, cozy home by wonderful people who took no notice of my obvious difference from them. It's not proper for me to join them at their table with an ungrateful heart. But it's too late to walk away. I inhaled and exhaled deeply, uttering a simple prayer as I did so.

"Are you alright, Hanna?" I opened my eyes upon hearing the worry in Naseema's voice.

"Yes, I'm good. Thank you." I smiled. "Can I help on anything?"

"No, no. You're a guest. Can I sit beside you?"

"Of course. Come." It's easy to be positive with the likes of Naseema around. Her cheerfulness was contagious. It saddened me to remember some of the comments I read from those travel blogs online about the Egyptians and Egypt. Perhaps they had not been as lucky as I was meeting this lovely family. Eslam entered the room with a bowl of what looked like pasta. It smelled really good. He took his seat across from me.

"What is it?" I always got excited at the sight of food, especially if I was trying it for the first time.

"It's called Koshari. It's made of rice, macaroni, and lentils."

"And this is Kebda, or liver, in English," his mom said upon joining us and taking the seat beside me.

When everyone was seated, we started to eat. Eslam's uncle asked how my vacation was going so far and the places I had seen. I shared the tour of the city I did yesterday.

"You're very brave to wander about on your own in our city. The tourists we had seen around here were always in groups or at least in couples."

"My friends, sadly, don't share my love for Egypt, so I had to come alone."

"I can't take that against them. Many said ours is not a safe country." The sadness in Eslam's voice was evident, though I couldn't be certain if it was because I refused his feelings or he was really talking about the ongoing conflicts in their country.

"There were people who were killed in their own homes. Safety is relative. Though I can agree with you that we can't take it against anyone if they don't want to come here for now."

"But what made you come to Egypt, Hanna?" Abdullah asked.

"I love Egypt." It was my usual reply when friends asked me why I was going there. "I have been fascinated and intrigued by your ancient history since a very young age. Your temples and monumental structures have not been equaled even with today's sophisticated and modern technology." I was beginning to enjoy the conversation as well as the food. Eslam's mom was a very good cook. I had never eaten liver before. I tried it today, and I found it surprisingly tasty.

"I'm glad you liked the simple meals we prepared, Hanna." There seemed to be no end to this woman's tenderness.

I reached for her hand and clasped it in both of mine. "Thank you for having me here. This is the very first time I have had a proper Eid celebration. I'll never forget this."

"We will not forget you too." Eslam reached out his right hand across to me. I gladly accepted it. To my surprise, the rest of them reached out as well and enveloped our hands with theirs. I was moved.

Expectedly, the farewell was difficult. More than anything, it was their kindness that touched me the most. All through my life, the people who had made a profound impact on me were those humble souls who had no bragging titles attached to their names. Yet the simple truth of their lives spoke so soundly in my heart.

*

At the train station, people were all eyes on me and Eslam. It made me feel uneasy. But not long after, an announcement was made asking passengers to be on the platform as the train to Cairo was approaching. Secretly, I sighed in relief. It's not a nightmare, but neither was it a dream I would have liked to stay on.

He walked me to the designated area for coach passengers. He looked down at me for a long while, seemingly trying to memorize my face. I kept fluttering my eyelashes out of discomfort. I found it very intrusive. Then he kissed me on the forehead and walked away without saying anything. I looked at him, walking fast amongst people with determined strides.

I'm sorry, Eslam.

The approaching train instantly infused excitement in me. *Tanta. Zaki. See you soon, my love.*

Once seated I felt the exhaustion today has brought. It sure was eventful. Nothing to regret, but the row with Eslam certainly was taxing, primarily because it wasn't expected. I hate being thrown off guard. It's a two-hour journey to Tanta. It's tempting to indulge in my thoughts about Eslam. Just then, I felt my phone vibrated inside my bag. I immediately took it out after remembering Zaki's message earlier.

Zaki: Hanna, where are you now?
Me: Just boarded the train.
Zaki: Just now? My…someone had enjoyed Egyptian Hospitality a lot today.

I got slightly irritated by his message. I opted not to respond. The true mark of a cultured lady was knowing when to restrain her tongue – or fingers – even when the mind was shouting curses. I put off the vibration of my phone, and just as when I was to put it back inside my bag, another message from Zaki popped in.

Zaki: Please head straight to Cairo. I'm already here. I'll Be waiting for you at the station.

Cairo? This sudden change of plan without explanation furthered my annoyance. I asked the guy seated across me for assistance since the ticket I held was only until Tanta.

"Excuse me, sir. I'm supposed to be headed to Tanta. But my friend said just now to go to Cairo directly. Can I have my ticket changed in Tanta and still remain on this train?"

"It's alright. Just say you asked for Cairo but you were given a ticket for Tanta instead. You're a tourist. You didn't know." And he smiled at me reassuringly.

It wasn't in my nature to lie or cheat, especially in instances where serious repercussions might follow. But I was too exhausted to think anymore or move from my seat for a new ticket. So as the train moved in the direction of Cairo, I allowed my thoughts instead to linger a bit in Alexandria, to Eslam.

I'm sorry, Eslam. Sorry.

I closed my eyes and fell asleep.

*

I awoke, sensing all the commotions around me. I asked the guy in the other aisle where we were. He said we would be reaching Cairo in less than 15 minutes. I checked my phone for any messages. There were three from Zaki, one in each hour, with the most recent just ten minutes ago.

Me: I'm about to reach Ramses station. Where do I meet you?
Zaki: I'll be right outside the main lobby of the station. Look for the steep, inverted pyramid pointing down from the ceiling.

Minutes after getting out of the train station, I found myself ten feet away from Zaki, his back on me. He's looking at the masterpiece in front of him. The inverted pyramid pointing down to a small replica of the pyramid in the Louvre in Paris was a lovely sight. People were stopping to take pictures of and with it. But it seemed to have faded into the background the moment I saw him. My first impulse was to run to him and hug him from behind. I hadn't seen him in the weeks leading up to the trip. He flew straight to Cairo after his business meetings in France. But I restrained myself and opted instead to just look at him at that distance. It was one of those times when I was hit with the reality that I was in love with this man. I took a step forward, and he turned around. His eyes immediately found me. When it's the heart that's looking, one could see faster and clearer. I smiled at him and slowly walked in his direction, taking in his beauty. He's walking faster with arms ready to take me in.

"Welcome to Egypt!" I loved the sense of security that his arms gave me. There's nowhere else I would rather be. The gentle kisses he planted on my cheeks turned my knees to gel-o.

"How was your train ride?"

"I was asleep on the entire journey. I was up quite early today." I couldn't stop smiling, and I was certain my cheeks were inflamed.

"You had made easy friends there, huh?"

"Your people are very nice and open. Everyone on the streets was either smiling or greeting me. I had a really good time up there in Alexandria."

"Looks like it." He pinched my cheeks.

"So, where to?"

"Let's drop your bags first at the hotel. Then – "

"At the hotel? I thought we would be staying at your apartment?"

"I'll explain once we're in the room. Come on." He offered his arm, and I hooked a hand on it. My mind was starting to sense something but I immediately dismissed all thoughts of worry. I knew the man I was with, and I had full trust in him from the start.

It was half an hour before we reached the hotel. There was not a single room available in all the hotels near Tahrir Square, so we had to travel all the way to the airport area, where he had me billeted at the Novotel. I was slightly dizzy with the way the driver handled the wheel. We were literally zigzagging on the road, and because there were no working seatbelts, I was tossed from side to side at the back until Zaki caged me in his protective arms.

"Remind me to not be here in Cairo when I'm pregnant!" He chuckled at my remark. I had to lean so close to his left ear to make him hear me say that. The noise and the wind outside discouraged talking.

Once we were in the room, I noticed its emptiness.

"Where are your things?"

"I need to go back to Tanta later. It's the first day of Eid. I don't want my mom to be alone."

I tried to mouth a response, but no sound came out. I was a bit sad at the thought of having to be on my own, but I couldn't afford to be upset, knowing full well what Eid means for Muslims.

"But how come I can't just stay at your place?"

"Security. You're safer here in the hotel."

There could be no other place safer than your arms.

"I'll come back tomorrow. We can visit the pyramids and the museum together," he said that with a wink and pulled me for an embrace. I inhaled deeply into his neck and filled myself with his scent. My head was getting foggy. He had a dreamy effect on me.

"Let me take a quick shower and change. I have had these clothes since morning." It's always a struggle for me to leave his arms.

"Be quick." He let me walk away with a kiss on the forehead, which made me hesitant to wash my face, childishly worried that doing so would erase the trace of it. Then I was reminded of Eslam's kiss at the train station. It hardly made an impact, though I knew it came from his heart.

It's sad when someone can't reciprocate our feelings. But the heart can't be forced to love another when it already has someone in it.

The sound of my body wash dropping to the floor put a break in my thoughts. I centered my mind on my actual task – scrubbing myself well – as if trying to cleanse away all of today's memory – Eslam's specifically.

The drive back to Tahrir Square was smooth, and we had relative privacy courtesy of the night and the tinted windows of the hotel service car.

"Where are we going?"

"It's a surprise." He winked at me, which caused my heart to flutter.

When we reached the city proper again, we got down in front of a small shop fronting the famous Nile River. Zaki spoke to the attendant. In minutes, we were being ushered into a waiting boat. It's big enough to carry about ten people, but we had it to ourselves and the boatman. On a full moon night, I was cruising in the most famous river in the world with the man I loved. What else could be more romantic than this? It's a memory that will forever be etched in my heart.

We talked about all that was happening in the office in Dubai and his last trip to France. He hinted at the stresses experienced there and the mountain of work waiting for him to attend to once this vacation was over.

We asked our boatman to take some pictures. We had brief exchanges with him. He was curious about my origin. In Dubai, I always seemed to confuse people, though it wasn't of my own making. My Asian facial features almost always have me mistaken for someone from either China or Korea, and at other times from Malaysia. But when they heard me talk, they paused, trying to determine my accent, and then would insist on knowing where I was from. It never failed to make me wonder myself as to how I really sounded like when I talked.

"I'm from the Philippines, sir." The boatman was quietly processing the information I shared with him. And as I had expected, he was not familiar with my country.

"Are you using a different map in this country?" I couldn't keep the bewilderment from my voice. Zaki laughed. I loved the sound of his laughter. Ours was a noisy world. Even my own mind could be so loud at times. His voice and his laughter could easily mute the entire world, making me only sensitive to him.

"I don't think that many Filipinos have visited our country." He went on to explain to the boatman in Arabic where in the world my country is located. The boatman nodding in recognition of what Zaki was saying. He stood to adjust the sail and we were left to ourselves again.

"Are you enjoying this?" He moved closer to me but was cautious of his actions as we were in public.

"Yes, very much so." I looked at him and smiled. "Thank you for this. This is very sweet of you. I have never been in a boat like this before. And we are cruising on the Nile! I had not expected this!"

He caressed my right cheek with the back of his left hand. The touch sent a sensation throughout my body. My desire was increasing with every touch, and I was certain it was the same for him. He may never have said anything this far, but his eyes and hands had communicated a lot to me.

The cruise took an hour. So far, it was the sweetest one hour I had ever had. Zaki extended his hand to help me leap from the boat.

"Hungry?"

"Famish." And I tried rolling my eyes to playfully support my claim.

"It never suits you." He tickled my side.

"Stop it!" I couldn't put force into my voice. His touches made me giddy way too much and way too easily.

"Why?" He was still attempting to land his fingers on my hips.

"You know what your touches do to me, Zaki." My cheeks were feeling hot, and my lips were curved into a smile.

"What does it do to you, Hanna?" He seemed to be in a romantic mood to keep playing this.

"Zaki, I'm serious. You need to stop. We are outside." Of course, I enjoyed his simple and seemingly innocent advances, and my fake denouncements were just to encourage him to continue. But this he knew, and so he never restrained himself, even at the beginning of our friendship.

"What would you like to eat?"

"I can't really think at the moment. Something light but filling enough would do." I wasn't feeling hungry. His very presence filled me up in all respects.

We walked around Tahrir Square. Four years ago, thousands of people filled this area, protesting against the leadership of President Hosni Mubarak and the alleged crimes of his administration. Tonight, the square was filled with people too, but because they were celebrating Eid. Zaki asked me if I wanted a picture with the two historic lions on one section of the square. The crowd of young Egyptians mounting and dismounting from the massive sculptures discouraged me.

The restaurant he wished us to dine at was closed. Surprisingly, so were many other shops. Only fast-food restaurants remained open.

"Do you mind?" He was pointing at Hardee's.

"Not at all." I think I can eat anything, even bugs cooked on raw fire, if the situation becomes dire, so long as we are together.

We talked about random things over our meals. Zaki's a joker. I always enjoyed our exchange of banters. But he was also as serious when the situation required it and especially about work. I deeply admired his professionalism. It's one of the things that I loved him for. He seemed to have a perfect balance in the way he conducted his life and his affairs. I knew there was still much for me to learn about him. What I had known so far had deeply enamored him to me.

After our dinner, we walked about in the streets surrounding the square. The people didn't seem weary of how late it was. Families with children and babies didn't seem vexed by the pollution and noise on the streets. The air had a merry note to it.

"The museum is right over there," Zaki interrupted my thoughts.

"What?"

"Where are you, Hanna?"

"I'm observing the people. Everyone seems happy as if your country is not beset with all sorts of troubles."

"Life must go on, Hanna. We, Egyptians, are simple people. Family and friends matter to us a lot. Yes, material things are essential to surviving the everyday rigors of life, and some luxuries would be good. But we are easily content. More than anything, I'm sure, what most of us have prayed and fasted for this past Ramadan was for this political drama to be over and things to become normal again."

I clung tighter to his left arm with both hands and planted a kiss on the back of his shoulder. I was aware that people were looking at us. My heart could ignore common decency sometimes. Zaki caressed my hand.

I loosened my grip on his arm when we neared the guards at the museum. Zaki spoke to them in Arabic.

"The museum opens at eight tomorrow and closes at three in the afternoon. Perhaps we can visit the pyramids first in the early morning, then come here after."

"That seems like a good plan." I smiled at him. It's easy to be cheerful and positive around the likes of Zaki. He was always positive himself, always cordial to people.

"Let's go back to the hotel. I still have to catch a train home." He offered his arm to me again, and as usual, I took it.

He hailed a taxi and informed the driver where we were headed before opening the passenger door for me. Once inside, he instinctively opened his arm to let me in. *My most favorite place.* Not even the most grandiose of palaces would do if he weren't there with me. He kissed me on the forehead. Zaki had never made an attempt to kiss me on the lips, not even treaded close to it. I was never bothered by it or had thought differently about it. He kissed my heart every day with his gentlemanly ways toward me.

"Are you sleeping?" He was gently running his thumb on my left cheek.

"No. I'm thinking."

"Thinking of what?"

"You." I detached my head from his shoulder and looked up at him. His green eyes seemed to be glowing in the dark. People looked at each other's eyes when they were talking. But not many could really see the other person. At that moment, as in many other times, I saw the man inside Zaki, the man I was in love with. I smiled at him and planted kisses on his jawline. Even I had no rushed desire to invade his lips. His left arm tightened around me, pressing me closer to him. That's how hearts made love to each other, through a passionate embrace. No clothes were shed, but both souls were naked. Both our eyes were closed, but both could see the other.

We didn't realize we had reached the hotel until the taxi had stopped. Zaki released me from his arms in order to pay our fare. He held out a hand for me when I was stepping out.

Arm in arm, we walked into the hotel and to my room. I was aware of the eyes walking with us. I was too happy to care.

Inside the room, we hugged each other again. In the privacy of that rented space, anything could have happened. If he had, even at the slightest, hinted that he wanted something sexual to transpire between us, I was certain I wouldn't resist. But Zaki, ever the gentleman, didn't even allow his hands to wander below my waistline. Mine own were content caressing his back and chest. Love didn't give us the license to do just whatever we wanted to do with each other.

"I would love to stay here with you." His forehead was gently leaning on mine.

"I would love that too. I missed you." I tightened my arms around him, meaning to convey the full extent of my emotion. Words could express only to a limited degree what I felt for Zaki.

"You know how important Eid is to us. Mom is alone at her house tonight. I do not…"

"I understand. You don't need to explain so much. You coming to see me and spending this wonderful evening together is enough. I love this night. Thank you, Zaki."

He pressed his lips on my forehead and let it stay there for some time, long enough for mine to feel it as well, sans the actual contact.

"What time would you like to go to the pyramids tomorrow?"

"It's up to you. How far is your place from here? And what time do you think you can leave tomorrow?"

"I'll have to check the timings of the train. I'll try to come as early as possible. So, by lunchtime, we would be in the museum. It would be so hot by then to still be outside."

"You're the boss." I winked at him, but both my eyes closed. He laughed.

"You're just so cute, Hanna! Your eyes can't do anything but just blink!" We both laughed.

It can appreciate beauty such as yours.

I looked at him for a while. I knew I could never get tired of looking at him.

"What are you thinking about?"

What else could I be thinking about? He was my frequent thought.

"You are always on my mind. You are always on my mind." I sang to him the lines of Elvis Presley's Always on My Mind. He wasn't the kind who blushed easily, but at that moment he did. I hit home.

"I better get going before my desires nail me completely here." He pulled me close to him once again for a quick embrace and then stood. I initiated the walk to the door. Respect had been at our core right from the start. I couldn't allow temptations to tarnish it. Love alone couldn't push two people forward. Feelings could come and go as the wind. Respect could give love more meaning, more depth.

I immediately closed the door after he stepped out and walked toward the elevators. The door served as a seal, trapping my desires that almost overflew from my emotional jar. I closed my eyes to steady myself. It's always a bit of a struggle to regain my equilibrium after separating from Zaki. I thought of watching the news to deviate my attention from him. Shortly after, sleep came and took me away from Egypt.

*

In the morning, the vibration of my phone woke me up. It was a message from Zaki. He couldn't come back to Cairo. Their relatives came for a visit, and his mother asked him not to go. The feeling this gave me was more foul than the taste of my unbrushed mouth. I felt sad. The ringing of the phone on my bedside table paused my morning drama.

"Hello." I pitied myself for the sadness I heard from my own voice.

"Good morning, ma'am. I just want to remind you that your service to go to Giza will be here in two hours."

Giza! The pyramids! How could I have forgotten? But I was wondering how they knew I wanted to go there.

"Am I going to be with a group?"

"No, ma'am. You'll be taken there alone by our contracted driver. Mr. Zaki arranged for it last night. He called us just now to remind us and to wake you up, too."

"I see."

"Do you want to have your breakfast in your room, ma'am?"

"No, thank you. I'll come down shortly. Thank you."

Oh, Zaki. I reached for my phone.

Me: Good morning, handsome! Thank you for arranging my ride to the pyramids. Very sweet of you to have done so. Kisses!
Zaki: You're welcome, beautiful! I'm sorry I can't join you. Our relatives are here. I can't just leave Mom to attend to them all.
Me: I understand. Don't worry about me. I'll be just fine.

Zaki: Take care, and enjoy! Keep me posted on your whereabouts.

And just like that, I was smiling again. My emotions were like a roller coaster ride. But I wouldn't have it any other way. Some people would be worth going for such a ride. Zaki was one of them.

After a quick shower, I blew my hair dry faster than I normally do. My stomach was growling from hunger, and my heart for adventure.

Buffet confused me. When there are a lot of options, it seems harder to choose.

But I must eat well enough to last until lunch or beyond.

I decided to go for the noodles and plain bread. I never like the idea of stuffing myself with a variety of food and risking having an upset stomach shortly after.

I checked the time on my watch. I still have half an hour. There's no English newspaper available. I went to the lounge area close to the front desk and went through the pictures I took from Alexandria. Not long after, a staff member approached me to tell me that my driver had arrived. I was instantly filled with excitement I had never before felt.

The driver could speak limited English, so there was hardly any conversation passed between us during the 40-minute drive to Giza. He had been briefed on where to take me. On the way, I snapped some pictures of the old but still beautiful mosques we passed by. There were many people on the streets. It was the second day of Eid, and so the celebrations were still at their peak. When we reached the bridge that crossed over the Nile River, the driver stopped on the side of the road. I asked him why we were stopping.

"For photo, ma'am. That's the river Nile."

"Oh, of course." I stepped out of the car and handed him my iPhone. After a few clicks, we resumed our journey.

When we entered Giza proper, I saw the apex of the biggest pyramid. My tears came on their own. My driver must have glanced at me from the rearview mirror and stopped when he realized I was crying.

"Madam, what's wrong?" Worry was evident in his voice.

"I'm alright. I'm just happy." I was drying my tears.

"But why are you crying if you're happy?" From worry his tone became baffled.

"This is a dream come true for me. I have longed to see the pyramids since I was a little girl."

He gave me the look a father would give to his daughter, with love and gentleness. "Don't cry, madam. The pyramids are beautiful. Have many pictures." And he stepped on the accelerator again.

Once we reached the visitors' registry, the driver spoke to someone who seemed to be the head of that office. He turned to me and asked, in a thick Egyptian accent, which I would prefer to ride on, a horse or a camel.

"A horse, please." After I paid, a guide was called to assist me mount on the horse. Immediately after being mounted, I made a clicking sound with my mouth to coach the horse to move. My eagerness couldn't be contained for much longer. My guide had to run after me, shouting behind me to slow down. I didn't listen to him. My heart was beating faster. Every stride of the horse was bringing me closer to my dream.

"Madam, you can't run this fast."

"Why is that?"

"You might fall off. You're not experienced."

Huh. That's what you think.

I kicked the horse on the side, and we sped in the direction of the pyramids. The guide kept shouting behind me. When a lady's running toward her dream, nothing and no one could stop her.

When I was finally in front of the pyramid of Menkaure, the smallest among the three, I pulled the rein on the horse to make it stop. I took a picture of it, both with my camera phone and with my eyes. I committed to memory this marvelous sight. After a few minutes, I willed myself out of the trance I was in. I again kicked the horse on the side, slightly this time, to push it to move. Each pyramid was at least five minutes apart from each other if one was riding a horse and it was running at quite a pace.

Upon reaching the tallest of the pyramids, the pyramid of Khufu, I felt obliged to unmount the horse and looked at it from the ground up. I felt a sense of great awe. It wasn't the tallest standing structure in the world anymore. But nothing could surpass its beauty, even now. Regardless of how sophisticated and modern the buildings of today are, the pyramids would remain one of the best and most enigmatic creations of man. Though many theorized that it was not man who built the pyramids, but other beings from outer space that came to our planet long before the very first humans existed. I didn't wish to concern myself with all that while there. Sometimes the best way to maximize an experience is to just enjoy something instead of questioning how it came to be.

I started climbing the pyramid, one boulder after the other. It sure was a challenge. The rocks were taller than me. My guide kept clicking shots. When I reached quite a height, the guard called on me to come down.

"My lady, please come down. No tourist has died here yet. Please don't be the first. Please come down now."

"Just a moment," I shouted back in response. I wanted to savor the chance to be there, be on the pyramid. This had been built thousands of years ago, and there I was, standing on its boulder, feeling its roughness against my hand, just how I had imagined it. I was awash with a feeling of immense happiness and pride. I just used to marvel at it on the glossy pages of the history books at school and in the pictures available on the internet. Now I was there. I looked about on the surrounding grounds. It was all sand. But I was certain that these sands hold buried secrets, the very greatness of this place. I recalled an artist's depiction in one of the books I read on how it must have looked like then. No wonder the greatest of conquerors had fought hard to have Egypt. It's remarkable even today, though looking desolate; what more then.

"My lady, please, come down now." I had to heed that or risk being asked to leave. My guide handed me back my phone when I reached the ground again. I didn't want to bother myself with the quality of the pictures he took right then. My eyes were recording everything anyway.

We moved to the next pyramid, the pyramid of Khafre. I followed my guide to the side of the pyramid where we left our horses. He walked ahead of me to the narrow entrance leading up to a room. There's a family inside, looking about and taking pictures. Once they were ushered out, I was allowed to have my time. I took pictures of every carving on the walls. I touched them. An extraordinary feeling of greatness came over me. I was living my dream. I was there, finally, after many years of dreaming about the place. This may not have been the actual tomb of the Pharaoh Khafre, but the room seemed to serve an important role in the pharaoh's burial preparations. I surmised that, looking at the carved drawings on the walls. I had been studying the history of the ancient Egyptians so I could somehow understand what the hieroglyphs on the walls were depicting.

When the new group of visitors came in, I took my leave. 15 minutes inside wasn't enough, but it would have to do for now. I could come back, and I would.

"Where do we go now?" I asked my guide upon remounting my horse.

"To the Sphinx." And he strode on. He was surprised to find me striding alongside him.

"How did you learn how to ride a horse?" I knew at some point he would ask me that.

"In Dubai. I attended some classes."

"How long was it?"

"10 hours."

"That short? You learned fast." I just smiled at him.

When we were close to the sphinx, he told me that we would have to go on foot to reach it. No animals were allowed anymore beyond a certain point. The heat was getting intense. It was summer, and I wasn't wearing the proper shoes that could withstand the heat of the sand. I refused to get off my horse. He just took pictures of me with the sphinx in the background. The distance was obvious, but the shot was good. He even managed to take some with the three pyramids behind me and the sphinx too.

I checked my watch. It had been two and a half hours since we commenced. I told him we should return. I was getting weary of the heat as well.

My driver was fast asleep on a bench under a tree. He was startled by the sound of our approaching horses.

"Madam, how was it?" He was smiling, as if his slumber had not been interrupted. Egyptians were such friendly people – and not only to tourists. As I had observed in Alexandria, while I went for my morning walk, everybody on the streets was greeting each other. In this aspect, they were similar to my people.

"I had a great time! I loved it there." He offered me a hand as I dismounted the horse.

"Good. Good. Come inside, have a drink."

I was served with the same drink that I had at Eslam's place. I gulped it down in one go. Out of my overwhelming excitement that morning, I forgot to carry a bottle of water with me.

"Madam, we must go. The museum will be closing soon." I checked my watch. It was half past one in the afternoon. The National Museum of Antiquities would be open only until three PM.

"You're right, sir. Let's go."

After saying our thanks, we left and drove back in the direction of Cairo. During then I thought of checking the pictures taken in the pyramids. There were messages from Zaki. I opted to go over it first.

Zaki: Hanna, where are you now?
Zaki: Hanna, bring a bottle of water with you. The Pyramid complex is big, and it's hot outside. And don't climb on it!

His last message made me chuckle. I had to respond.

Me: I did! I climbed the pyramid of Khufu! The guard was horrified!
Zaki: For sure he would be! Oh Hanna, always so mischievous! Where are you now?
Me: We're heading to the museum now. How are things with you there?
Zaki: My mouth's tired from all the talking since this morning! We just had lunch. Have you had yours?
Me: Not yet; perhaps after the trip to the museum. I'm not hungry.
Zaki: Wow! That's new. You're always hungry. You must be enjoying yourself so much that you're forgetting food.

That message was capped with a laughing emoji, to which I responded the same.

Zaki: But at least drink something. It's very hot today. And Hanna, don't take pictures inside the museum. It's not allowed.

That last note made me frown. I would love to have pictures of the mummies and their sarcophagi; even one would suffice. But the thought of being asked to leave if I get caught, or worse, be arrested, made my hair stand on end. And I was certain Zaki would hang me upside down! *Write*. I hurriedly searched my bag, trying to see if I had a pen and anything to write on. I was elated to find inside my pocket notepad.

Giza was more than 30 minutes' drive from Cairo. I was feeling pangs of hunger, but I didn't want to miss the chance to see the Museum of Egyptian Antiquities. It was my last full day in Egypt. The following day, Zaki and I would be flying back to Dubai in the afternoon. I gulped down the entire content of the bottled mineral water I was given at the registry. It should keep me feeling full for at least an hour more.

When we reached the museum, my driver went down and opened my door, as I was still counting the loose bills on my hand to tip him. He then offered his hand and assisted me out. He thanked me warmly for employing his services. His gesture astonished me. The kindness of strangers never failed to touch my heart.

After I paid my entrance fee at the gate, I walked toward the museum. There were people offering their services to tour and guide me to understand the collections inside. With the exception of the Egyptologists, I could challenge anyone's knowledge on the history of the ancient Egyptians. I could even read the hieroglyphs, though not as fast or as accurately, for the earliest Egyptians didn't have just one set of alphabets. Some letters were represented by more than one character. Words were spelled – or expressed – using symbols in combination with other characters in order to describe or explain something. So, one must analyze the other characters in order to determine what was being said in one entry carved on the walls, columns, and sarcophagi where the mummies were kept after they had been embalmed.

The museum was a soft pink building with a small dome on top and an arch opening with carved statues of their ancient goddesses, reminiscent of Roman influence. In front were the replicas of the sphinx and the statue of Tutankhamun. On the grounds were statues of animals revered by the ancient Egyptians and other carved artifacts. The camera was strictly prohibited inside. I had to commit everything to memory, beginning at the door.

The first level displayed items reflecting the last dynasties that ruled Egypt. The sarcophagi and some mummies of the royal family, along with the belongings they were discovered with, were on the same floor. Thousands of other ancient artifacts could be found there, including decaying papyruses, coins used during trade, large life-like structures of pharaohs, and replicas of boats used while traversing the river Nile. The second level had the jewelry used by the pharaohs and their families, along with other important items used during their time. It took me a full three hours to browse through the entire collection.

I couldn't ignore my deepening hunger, and so I retraced the steps Zaki and I took last night. I saw a KFC chain and decided to go for it. I cleared my plate in 15 minutes flat. I thought of going to the Khan el Khalili bazaar, but the nearly three hours of horse ride inside the pyramid complex under the Egyptian summer sun was starting to take its toll on my body. I went back to the hotel for a nap. It stretched into a deep sleep. I awoke at nine in the evening. I hurriedly took a shower and changed. Shortly before ten, I was at the reception and asked the front desk for a driver to go back to town.

"Madam, it's ten o'clock in the evening," disbelief was evident in his voice and face.

"I know. But I'm leaving tomorrow, and I have not bought any souvenirs yet."

"How do you wish to go there, a normal taxi or the hotel service?"

"Is there a way you can contact my driver earlier?"

"I can try." Shortly after he was on the phone with my driver. "He'll be here in 15 minutes, madam."

"Okay, good. Shukran."

Not long after, my driver arrived, looking sleepy. But his usual friendliness was still there.

"Good evening, madam."

"Good evening! Thank you for coming out for me again."

"It's okay. Happy to drive you. But why so late, madam?"

"I fell asleep. I just woke up an hour ago."

"Me ready to sleep." And he laughed.

"Oh, I'm sorry! You shouldn't have come anymore. Can you still drive?"

"Yes, yes. No worry." He smiled and stepped on the accelerator.

We drove in relative silence. I wished to keep him engaged in conversation to prevent him from falling asleep while driving. But I was also worried that doing so might interrupt his concentration on the road. I decided to just stay alert instead. His car was relatively new, and the seatbelts were working, so I strapped myself in.

There was traffic near the bazaar. A huge crowd was still gathered outside the nearby mosque, blocking the parking spaces. We had to park at least 15 minutes away. I had curious eyes following me as we walked toward the entrance of Khan el Khalili. My driver was very protective, walking very close behind me and sometimes waving the others out of my way. Eager storekeepers crowded around me, trying to outsmart each other by offering their goods at bargain prices. We walked into one shop, and I was given a bottle of mineral water. They had very nice merchandise but very pricey. I was secretly seeking my driver's approval regarding the price. We had no prior understanding on the matter, but he seemed to have sensed I would need his assistance on it. He paid no significant regard to the few items I checked at the first store, so I took that as disapproval on his part. We moved on.

After checking a few stores, we found the same items I liked but at cheaper prices at a store almost at the intersection with another street within the bazaar. I got the bust of Nefertari, the wife of the legendary Ramses The Great, and small canopic jars with the heads of Horus' sons, along with some other knick-knacks for friends. I bought the necklace made from sapphire stones set on gold-plated metal I saw hanging by the door of his shop as well. It was simply exquisite. When I was about to pay, a considerable-sized pyramid made from granite stone caught my eye. It was by the counter side.

"It's not for sale, ma'am. It belonged to my great-grandfather. This store was handed down to my grandfather, then to my father, and now to me."

"Do you have anything similar to this?"

"No, ma'am. That was made from pure granite, commissioned by my great-grandfather when this shop was built." The weight of the item in my hands proved that to me. After all these years, though the original gold color used to emphasize the engravings was fading, the engravings themselves had remained intact. I carefully put the pyramid statue back where it had been standing and noticed that the space it occupied had a different color on that counter. He wasn't exaggerating about its age.

"Thank you. It's beautiful." I didn't understand why I was sad, but I couldn't hide my emotion.

When we stepped out of the shop, a group of Egyptian teenage girls approached us and asked me something in Arabic. I didn't understand them, so I looked at my driver for clarity.

"They want to have a photo with you, madam."

"But why is that? I'm not a celebrity."

"Yes, but you're a tourist." He smiled and held out his hand to get the camera phone from one of the girls. They all stood on both sides of me while my driver did a few clicks.

I thanked them in Arabic, and they giggled. One of them touched my hair and asked if it was real. *Does it look fake?* I didn't know the proper response, so I just smiled. My driver spoke to them in Arabic, and he excused both of us. I asked him why they seemed so fascinated with my hair. He said my hair was like that of Cleopatra, their last woman pharaoh – thick, deep black, and very straight. That was flattering for me. I wasn't sure if hers was real, though, as history suggested, they wore wigs then. The ancient royalties of Egypt shaved the hair all over their bodies as part of their hygiene. But then I remembered that Cleopatra was not a pure Egyptian.

We were ready to take our leave when the shop owner called out to me. He handed me a small cloth bag, and in it was the granite pyramid of his great-grandfather.

"Why?" My voice sounded of confusion and excitement.

"It had been here for so many years. We had not paid so much thought to it, neither had the many tourists who came to my shop, except you. This pyramid will be better preserved if it's in your hands. Here, it just collects dust. My great-grandfather would be happy, I know, that someone who has the same taste as him would care for this."

It wasn't customary for them to embrace a complete stranger, more so if that stranger was a woman. But I was compelled by my instinct to do so. I bridged the physical distance between us. He was taller than me, and so he leaned down to take me into his arms.

"Thank you. This is very sweet of you. I'll take very good care of this. I promise."

"I know, sister. And my great-grandfather would be smiling down upon you for that." He gave me a kiss on the top of my head, and we went about our way.

Heading to our car, a group of young men was running toward our direction and had my driver not pushed me further to the side of the street, they would have collided with me. That suddenness pulled me completely back to the present times. The weight of the pyramid in the bag I was carrying had a dreamy effect on me.

The drive back to the hotel was quicker. Traffic had greatly subsided given how late it was. After I thanked my driver, I went straight to my room. The huge pool was inviting, but I was eager to examine my purchases. I took some pictures and sent them to Zaki.

Zaki: It's very late. Why are you still up?
Me: I just came back from the bazaar. I bought some Souvenirs for myself and my friends.
Zaki: You were in town this late at night? Hanna, what were you thinking? What if something had happened to you?
Me: Nothing happened to me, Zaki. So just chill, please. My driver earlier to the pyramids was the same one who accompanied me to Khan el Khalili.

He didn't respond anymore. I was certain I would hear from him about tonight's escapade tomorrow at the airport. I shrugged at the thought. It's typical of Zaki to admonish me but he always does so in a loving manner. It's one of the many things I found so endearing about him.

*

The night passed quickly. My alarm went off at seven in the morning. I had a shower and went down for breakfast. The restaurant was still quiet, with just a few guests scattered about in the huge dining area. I chose a table at the far end with a view of the garden and pool. I faced the crowd so as not to seem aloof. Since yesterday's breakfast, I noticed that there was a good mix of guests of Europeans and Arabs. I searched for other Asians. I was the only one. It didn't make me feel uncomfortable. Even amongst my friends, my choices of places to visit vary greatly. I love archaeology and history – the more ancient, the better. My thoughts were interrupted by the vibration of my phone. It was a message from Zaki.

Zaki: Good morning, Hanna! What time will you be at the airport?
Me: Good morning handsome! I'm very close to the airport. I did an online check-in too. So, perhaps two hours before the flight should be okay.
Zaki: See you then.

I walked around the hotel after breakfast. People were just waking up. Elevators kept pinging, and their doors opening and closing constantly. I checked my watch. It was just eight in the morning. Still no English newspapers, so I opted to go back to my room. I would have to settle for CNN on television.

I was arranging my luggage when my phone vibrated again by the bedside table. I picked it up to see a message from Eslam. I was slightly irritated. I would rather forget about him. I pressed my thumb against the button to unlock my phone.

Eslam: Hi Hanna. What time is your flight today? I'm in Cairo. Can I see you before you leave?

The message made me feel crossed. *Why would he be in Cairo?* I didn't want to be rude, but I wasn't up to answering him. I put the phone back on the table, and I resumed what I was doing. Not long after, my phone buzzed again.

Eslam: Please don't be angry anymore, Hanna. I just really want to see you again. I just want to talk to you. Please.
Me: Hi Eslam. I'm sorry, but I cannot meet you anymore. I'm with him.

I was certain that would shatter him. But he left me with no other choice. Kindness sometimes encourages people to push you further in the direction you do not want to go. I continued packing and decided to ignore the phone should it alert again. I missed so much of the news. I looked for the BBC. The news may be depressing for some, but I could not last a day without knowing what was going on in the world. I stopped fidgeting with the remote when there was a broadcast on Syria. In the footage, the camera and the reporter shook as a bomb hit the ground. I was reminded of Eslam once more and realized the effects of my words to him might be similar. I closed my eyes. *I'm sorry, Eslam.* The heart could not be stopped when it wanted someone, but neither could it be forced to like another.

When the clock hit ten, I stepped out of my room. Our flight was at half past 12 in the afternoon. My hotel was a mere ten minutes away from the airport. There was a free shuttle service, so I was delivered straight to the departure gate. To my horror, Eslam was there. It's needless to ask why. I was upset, and my mind had instantly formed sentences that could burn him down to ashes in five seconds.

"Hi, Hanna. Please don't be angry. I'm not trying to be creepy. Just hear me out, please." He was pleading like a kid, but it's not working on me. "I just wanted to see you again before you go. I don't know if I will see you again after today. Please, Hanna, talk to me." He was standing very close to me, with eyes burning with both desire and longing. My eyes were wandering about, searching for Zaki.

"He's inside, having coffee, and working on his laptop." My eyes widened in disbelief. I never showed him a picture of Zaki. "We, Egyptian men, are very sensitive. Looking at him, I can tell he's your type. He's wearing a red hooded jacket."

True enough, Zaki was wearing a red jacket with a hood. He was typing on his laptop. I looked around before approaching him. He looked different than most Egyptian men there. He had a more worldly appeal. His aura emitted more confidence. There was more class to his general appearance, having traveled the world for years.

I glided toward his direction and placed both my hands on his shoulders. He knew my touch and looked up at me with smiling eyes. I leaned down and planted a kiss on his forehead. I just saw him the other day, but I seemed to have missed him so much.

"Hi, beautiful." He stood to give me a peck on both cheeks and a quick embrace.

"I love your scent," I said after we pulled away. "What are you doing just now?"

"There are emails that cannot wait for responses anymore. I might need to accompany the guys for their next assignment in a refinery in the south of Hungary."

"We're not even back to the office yet, Zaki." I should be used to his hectic and ever-busy work schedules by now. Since last year, Zaki had been to seven different countries for meetings with customers and works in the refineries with his team. Yet my heart could not get used to his absence.

"This is how I earn my living, Hanna." And just like that, he went back to his emails. His dedication to work was an admirable trait I loved about Zaki. He was utterly serious and focused. Since joining the company nine years ago, he had not had a relationship proper enough to be considered so.

I let him work to pass the time while I opted to continue with the book I was reading. Eslam had completely slipped out of my mind until I caught him in my peripheral vision. I looked in his direction. He was standing by a souvenir shop, looking intently at me and us. The pain was evident on his face. I looked at Zaki, consumed with work. I told him I would just look around.

I stood and started walking toward the opposite direction of where we were. I saw Eslam walking in the same way. I stopped at another souvenir shop leading to the gates of departing passengers.

"Hanna…"

"What do you want?" Irritation was all over me. "Why did you come here? What do you want?"

"Hanna, please don't be angry. I just wanted to see you again." I could hear the sincerity in his voice, and his face conveyed the same tact.

"Well, now you see me." I was looking at him straight and square, my irritation still at its peak. He didn't speak for a full minute, just standing there, staring at me. I didn't remove my eyes from him as well. I wanted to see through this and be done with it.

"I think I'm in love with you, Hanna. He's such a lucky guy. But I can see why you love him. He seemed – "

"Oh, for goodness sake, don't make a scene here." I snarled at him. Such childish acts have never elicited any good reaction from me. I got irritated when people started to show so much more emotion than what the situation actually called for – especially in public. I had always been controlled in displaying my feelings when outside. I expected the same from people, though I knew it was an absurd request.

He looked up, probably to make the tears go back in or to ask for some help from heaven. I started to walk back to the coffee shop. He didn't stop me. He wouldn't be able to anyway. I had made it perfectly clear in Alexandria that I couldn't reciprocate his feelings. Once I was back at the table with Zaki, he remarked about my cheeks.

"Did you just run? Your cheeks are burning."

"Yeah, quite a walk it had been." Life and its many surprises always caused my cheeks to turn crimson. I closed my eyes and made a silent resolution to never think of Eslam again after that day.

I'm sorry. I didn't wish to be a painful memory for you.

"Hanna?" I didn't hear him. It was his touch that pulled me out of my own mind. "Are you okay?" He moved his chair closer to me and draped one arm on my shoulders.

"Yes, I'm good. Just feeling tired with all that had happened on this trip." I rested my head on his shoulder. He gave me a kiss on the forehead. Those were some of the sweetest things I had experienced in my life.

"I think we better go to our gate. It should be open now." I didn't move right away. I wanted to stay by his side, be enveloped by his scent. A woman's place was beside her man, regardless of where in the world that would be. I was in my place, and I wanted to relish it for as long as I could.

"Hanna?" I remained motionless beside him; eyes closed. He caressed my cheek with the back of his hand. I love shared tenderness like this. Priceless. He tickled my side. It elicited a reaction from me. I opened my eyes, smiling. "Let's go." Reluctantly, I disentangled from his arm.

On the way to the departing gates, my eyes wandered about, searching for Eslam, silently wishing he had left. I was certain Zaki wouldn't feel threatened by him, but I didn't want the two of them to cross paths. The former's reaction was what I was more concerned about. When we had checked in and entered the waiting lounge, I felt totally at ease and relaxed. Only passengers could be in that area. The nightmare was officially over. I resumed my reading while Zaki was playing on his iPad. Not long after, we were ushered in for boarding.

Zaki was sleeping during the flight. I was tired, but I couldn't fall asleep. For some reason, I was agitated. Emirates had a good selection of movies to watch onboard, but none appealed to me. I switched off the screen. The slight buzzing in my ears from being up in the air discouraged me from reading. I looked at Zaki. He still looked handsome, even when asleep. I was so tempted to kiss him but was worried that I might wake him. I looked at him for a long time, running my eyes to the outline of his jaws, his full lips, his nose, his long eyelashes that flickered so beautifully when he spoke, and his thick but trimmed brows. He was a beautiful man. And the kindness of his heart furthered his appeal. I could look at him every day, forever even. I knew that even when we got older, I would still see that beauty I saw then. The heart had eyes that could see better, deeper, and longer. I loved this man, and I knew then that I always would, come what may.

I fell asleep halfway through the flight. I dreamed that I was standing in front of the pyramid of Khufu, dressed in a flowing long white frock. No movement, no sound, and there was no one else there. Then smoke started to come out of me, from my body. I was burning, and the wind was making the flames grow, consuming me completely. But I wasn't moving. I was burning inside out but standing there motionless. And I was crying; my face was drenched with tears. I awoke very startled, and my chest heaving. I swallowed hard to clear the buzz from my ears. Zaki was still sleeping. I hooked my right arm to his left and laid my head on his shoulder. He moved and leaned his head on top of mine. My heart was still working double time inside me. The sight of me burning was on full display on the screen in my mind.

"Are you okay?" I didn't realize that he had noticed my anxiety.

"I had a dream. It was disturbing." He kissed me on the head, and I inched closer to him. His arms were my sanctuary. What I wouldn't give to stay in it all the time.

We were quiet on the way home. It's obvious that there were matters weighing heavy on his mind, so I left him to them. The startling feeling the dream gave me still shadowed me, keeping my lips sealed too. I made a mental note to search its meaning on Google upon reaching home. The taxi driver pulled over outside his building in Marina.

"See you tomorrow in the office." He kissed me on the forehead, as usual.

Chapter 5

"How long will you be in England?" That was the second time he had asked me the same question on the same day.

"Just for two weeks," I answered without looking at him. I was doing a final check of my boss' PowerPoint presentation for his next trip to the head office.

"When are you leaving?"

"Zaki, we spoke about this not long ago. Try to remember."

"I'm hoping that your answer will change each time I ask." I looked at him, and he winked at me before walking away. I was left with a warmth that traveled down to my toes. How easy it was for him to affect me.

I continued on with my task when my phone vibrated. It was a message on Facebook Messenger from my brother Henry in England.

Henry: All set for your trip here?
Me: Yes, Kuya (older brother). I'm ready.
Henry: Send me a copy of your tickets, please, so I know what time to pick you up at the airport.
Me: I'll do so shortly. I'm at work, finishing up an important report for my boss.

An hour before work was over, Zaki came over to my desk. I was listing the things I wanted to bring for my trip to the UK.

"Was this trip planned?"

"What do you mean?" I understood his question, but I wanted to be certain of his point.

"I thought you wanted to see the countries in the region first. How come England, then?"

"My older brother Henry invited me over. I couldn't say no. I've always wanted to see England."

"But there is no occasion of any kind for this invitation, just that he wants you to come over, is that right?" I wasn't sure where this conversation was leading, but I was certain Zaki was up to something. I just couldn't grasp it then.

"No, there's nothing specific about this visit. He just thought it would be a good idea to do it now because it's summer there, it's not as cold." I stood, placed my hands around his neck, and started to gently caress him. "You seem rather anxious. What are you thinking about?"

"Nothing. I'm just going to miss you. Two weeks is too long." He pulled me closer to him and buried his face in my hair. I didn't miss out on the sincerity in his words. But I felt something else with it too. As always, my mind wasn't on a high scale when I was this close to him, so I failed to put a hand on the matter that was seemingly pressing heavily in his mind.

When we heard someone approaching, we pulled away. Not that office romance was prohibited. By now, I was certain that our colleagues were more than aware that there was something between us. None of them had asked either of us directly, though, not that they needed to anyway.

"Excuse me guys, I just need something from Hanna." Zaki, half-sitting on my desk, stood and walked away after shaking Saad's hand, our Syrian manager.

"Yes, Saad, how can I help you?"

"I sent you the layout for the roll-up banner I will need for the exhibition next month. Please coordinate with our local supplier for it."

"Alright, I'll get into it." My eyes were locked on the screen before me, but I failed to focus. Zaki's behavior baffled me. Just as when I thought I knew him a bit better, this situation was proving me wrong.

The moment the clock hit six in the evening, my internal bell was ringing. I managed to study the layout Saad sent me and forwarded the same to our local supplier. I checked my notebook, and there were no tasks I had scheduled for today which I wasn't able to complete. But during the last hour, I nearly had to beat myself up to regain my concentration.

*

While in bed that night, sleep was elusive. My mind was still preoccupied with thoughts of Zaki. Something was bothering him, and it had something to do with me. This, in turn, started to bother me.

My flight was the following weekend. It would be my first time in England. My older brother, Henry, and his family had been living there for over 20 years. I had always nurtured a silent desire to roam the streets of London and see the magnificent castles in the country. I was excited at the thought of another dream coming true. But in my throat was a lump, so to speak, that was causing me discomfort emotionally.

Zaki had been away on business trips for most of the first months of this year. Last year, he traveled to seven countries in three different time zones, with repeated visits to some countries in the region and in the head office in France. WhatsApp was our only tangible link apart from those sporadic emails he sent pertaining to changes on his overseas trips. So, it wasn't like we would be separated for the first time. But he gave me the impression that it would be the start of our permanent separation. This thought pressed hard on my consciousness.

*

"Good morning, handsome!" I stood up from my chair the moment I saw him. I barely slept the night before. The thought of seeing him in the morning was what made me overcome the bed today. There's no one else in the office yet. We lingered longer than usual in each other's arms. I noticed how particularly sentimental his actions of late, how he didn't seem to want to let me go when we were embracing. He's more physical, and there was a tinge of sadness to his touches. It flustered me. But each time I asked him, I received a nonchalant response. "Did you have a good sleep?" I was caressing the growing stubble on his jaw.

"Not until you're beside me." The look in his eyes was melting me. It would be hard to outsmart me, but his very presence alone could shut up my logic. I always seemed lost for words around Zaki. He didn't challenge my vocabulary. On the contrary, he was making me feel the meanings of words by defining love with his actions. He made me appreciate the sensation of touch with his gentleness. He made me hear his unspoken words by merely looking at me.

"You disarm me so easily with your sweetness. Do you realize that?" I tiptoed to reach his cheek. He leaned down a bit and kissed me on one cheek too, his lips tantalizingly so close to my lips.

"You, on the other hand, have a way of paralyzing me almost every time. I don't want to do anything else when I'm around you. I can't think about work. I can't function properly." He covered me with both arms, full body hug, my heart beating hard against his. I had never been embraced in such a way, nor would I want to ever be again by anyone else. That moment was perfection in its sweetest sense.

I looked up to him. His eyes were smiling at me. I was in love with this man, and I knew then that I always would be.

"Let me go to my desk and do some work before your charms nail me here." And he fled after giving me a kiss on the forehead.

What a way to start the day! I didn't have to check myself in the washroom. I was certain that my cheeks were inflamed. I was left inside our bubble, still steaming with heat from our exchanges. The voice of the biometric machine outside our main door ushered someone in. I straightened my dress and coat and tacked my hair behind one ear.

"Good morning, Hanna. Wow, your cheeks are really red! Did you just get in here too? It's boiling outside." That's our ever-observant but friendly engineer from Kuwait who we fondly call Eli.

"Yeah, I'm feeling a bit hot this morning." *Though not from the sun*, I almost added. I walked with him to the pantry to fetch a glass of water. He exchanged pleasantries with Zaki on the way.

The day went by quite fast, with me constantly inside the boss's office, planning and discussing with him the entire agenda of his trip and the presentation he was scheduled to give. But there was a shadow at the back of my mind, standing very still and was seemingly waiting for the perfect time to come face-to-face with me.

*

"I remember you told me before that your dream husband is either an English or an Aussie man. Perhaps he's worried that you would meet someone while there." Lana's thought was amusing, but I wasn't tickled. "Girl, stop overthinking. Just like what he said, maybe he's just going to miss you."

I was certain it was more than that. There's a strong current swaying back and forth inside my heart, threatening to shift my equilibrium. But the direction from which the storm was coming from was still unknown to me.

"Let's go home, Lana. There's still work tomorrow." We left the café after settling our dues. I wanted to be home, to be alone with my thoughts, in order to confront the shadow lurking in the dark alley of my consciousness.

Upon reaching my apartment, I changed into my exercise outfits. I was determined to think through the matter so I could deal with it better. I was in the middle of my hula hoop spinning session when a thought stopped me on my track. It was just two months back when I went to Egypt with Zaki. My brother's invitation must have something to do with that. He didn't even ask if I could go on leave immediately after my last trip. His was more of a summon, though subtle it may seem. I was starting to feel more uneasy. Emotions were brewing inside me, a mixed, intense concoction.

I switched off my music player which was still blasting in my ears. My chest was rising up and down heavily because of the mad drumming of my own heart. *What's this?* The phone in my hand vibrated. It's a message on WhatsApp from Zaki.

Zaki: Hanna, are you still awake?

I was beyond awake. I was starting to get on fire! I replied with a curt yes and a smiley. In less than a minute, there came another message from him.

Zaki: Do you want to take a walk?

It was half past the hour of nine in the evening. But the concept of time didn't exist in love.

Me: I'm actually already dressed for that. I'll meet you in front of my building, say in ten minutes? Or that's too soon for you?
Zaki: I'm all geared up myself. I'll jog going to your place. See you in ten minutes, then.

Ashley's question startled me as I was heading for the door. She's still up binge-watching on Netflix.
"Going somewhere, babe?"
"I'll just take a walk with Zaki."
He didn't disappoint. At nine minutes and 43 seconds, he entered my cluster, looking all warmed up. Had I not moved

to JLT, it wouldn't have been possible for us to meet at this late hour.

"A man of your words, indeed, sire." I had both arms open while standing at the top of the stairs by my building's entrance. He came into my welcoming arms and gave me a slight squeeze. And as had been our habit, we locked eyes for some time before pulling away.

"Are you alright?" I couldn't hold my tongue. My eyes saw something like a glint of sadness in his.

"I'm okay, though I'm feeling edgy somewhat these days."

"I noticed that. Do you want to talk about it?"

"Sure. I actually want to ask you about your trip."

I had an inkling it would be our topic.

"What about it?"

"Does your family know anything?"

I didn't really have to say anything. The photos of us I uploaded on Facebook would speak for themselves.

"What do you mean exactly?"

"Do your brothers know who I am? And who am I to you?" That should have been easy enough for me to answer. But somehow the words pooled at my throat and almost made me choke. We stopped shortly after and sat on a bench, away from the pathway of the crowd.

His question made me think harder than I previously have had in relation to him. My older brother, Hector, knew of my feelings for Zaki. We spoke about him now and again. My other brother, Henry, on the contrary, never asked me anything about him. Regardless, I was certain of my feelings for Zaki. He's the man I loved. However, this world required that people put labels on everything – from storage containers to relationships. It's the logical way of life. But should it be the same with love? Should love follow certain rules or formats for how to be?

"We haven't really defined who we are to each other. But I'm sure you know who you are to me and where you stand in my life."

That wasn't really the answer he wanted to hear. He knew who he was to me. But I couldn't word my responses right just then, so I opted to direct them in the way where I hoped I could stumble on the right answers.

"I care so much about you, Zaki. I love what we have. I'm happy, and I can't remember being this way before. I know it's necessary to define what is this that we have and what we are doing. But work had pulled you away from me for much of these times. I didn't want to add pressure on you. And to be quite frank, I don't really care about taping a label on us. In your own way, you've made me feel secure enough."

Again, not the answer most fitting to his question, but it's true. The people around us, I was sure, had been wondering what's the real score between us. Lana had been on me on this matter for almost since this affair took flight. My other friends were on the same wagon, jokingly coaxing me to admitting each time we dined out. I had always managed to evade them. Tonight, though, Zaki's words had me against the wall, so to speak.

"You've been very patient with me on this, Hanna. I'm ashamed of myself for not being more upfront about this early on."

There's really no need for him to be embarrassed about this. I let the situation drag on in the absence of a definite direction. Not that I was afraid of where it could lead to, but more so because I was just not as concerned about naming this relationship. I never believed in it, nor was there a need to do so. I have had relationships where boundaries were defined but love was an insufficient supply. Almost all of my boyfriends had expressed a desire to marry me, but not all of them seemed invested enough in that enterprise. Being of age and with a more mature mind and heart, my outlook on men and relationships dramatically differed.

"My father might be twisting in his grave for the way I'm handling this situation with you. But you're right. Work had been very hectic for me. You know my schedules. You plan it with me, all my trips, everything. But still, I know I should have been more communicative about us, about what we are. I do think about you almost all the time. Even from a thousand miles away, I keep you close to my thoughts. Your happiness matters to me, Hanna." That last sentence gently pinched me inside. I reached for his hand, found it, and he enveloped mine with both of his.

"I know what you're trying to tell me. I can't find the right words to express it, but I do understand. That's why I never let it bother me. When the heart understands, the mind follows eventually."

"But we need to do something, do we not? In order for the people around us to better understand what we have."

"Why do we need to make it our business for others to understand our business?" I had always been guarded about my relationships. I kept a lot more inside than I let people in. My heart's not a public office where people could sit and debate about its affairs.

"Definition. Every word has its definition in the dictionary, just as everything else in this life."

I had to hold my tongue behind my teeth. He's trying to sort out our situation, trying to put a more concrete structure to it, so I should stay shut and be patient.

"I'm sure your family's wondering about all those photos you have of us on your Facebook. Just as my mother would be if she were to see them. My sister had started to ask. So perhaps it's time we define us."

"But you Muslims do relationships differently. How do you propose we do this?" My heart was starting to race. My mounting nervousness caused me to lose control over my tongue. That question had been on my mind all this time. I never attempted to search for an answer because I knew it wasn't up to me.

"Do you think you can live with someone like me all your life?"

I wouldn't lose sleep if world leaders would migrate the entire population to Mars and leave me and him alone to be stewards of the earth. But take him away from me, and not a single planet in our universe, or any other, would be habitable for me. Life would simply cease to be.

"I wouldn't want to live it otherwise."

He pulled me for an embrace and rewarded me with a kiss on my forehead. His lips lingered there for a while.

"You will not regret it." I looked up at him with glistening eyes, tears at the ready. My bosom was enlarged and expanding with every minute since. It's a promise I knew I could hold on to. For the first time in my life, I believed that someone really loved me.

"One more workday tomorrow. Come on, let me walk you back home." It's a slow walk back to my building. We almost didn't want to separate. If it had been the weekend, I was certain we would continue the stroll on to his neighborhood and all the way to the beach area. The heart could walk for miles and miles if it was alongside the one it loved.

"Quite a walk, huh?" I said teasingly.

"Never a dull moment with you, Ms. Lee."

"I can say just about the same for you, Mr. Al-Hamid." He gave me another tight hug and a lingering kiss on the forehead. I knew it would always be like this for us. Oh, what a journey it would be!

*

Over lunch, I shared with my female colleagues what transpired the night before. Roshie was particularly giggly.

"Did you kiss?" I motion my head to mean no while mouthing a spoonful of pasta.

"No? How come?" Kaycee asked with a mouth full of her cooked Adobo and rice. How best to answer her?

Zaki and I had shared a very close friendship for nearly three years. We had grown familiar with the contours of each other's bodies when we embraced. He knew too well to what degree he would angle his head to allow mine enough space to cradle against his neck. We would sit down with our knees always touching or our lower torsos aligned side by side. If we were with our team, he'd be on the exact opposite seat from me, so *"I can always look at you,"* as he would always say. My forehead and cheeks were well accustomed to the softness of his full lips, and my hands to the feel of his. All of me had been well integrated with all of him. We loved each other. We didn't need to verbalize it. Love required expression, not pronouncement. And though a kiss on the lips was a usual gesture to show one's love to another, I was never bothered that we still hadn't done so. On the contrary, I found it added a thrill to our relationship and gave us both something to look forward to.

"Well, do we really need to kiss?" They responded in affirmative unison, which surprised me. "Why?"

"Why not? People in love kiss each other," Joan said, Zaki's commercial assistant.

"Well, we haven't. And I'm perfectly alright with that – for now." I didn't doubt the feelings of Zaki for me, and I wouldn't allow the murmurings of the world to change that.

"Do you think it's because of their religion?" Roshie looked both serious and concerned.

"No. Here, there are so many people who are in interfaith relationships. I'm sure all of them are kissing each other, or maybe more." Another point for Joan for that.

A thought came to me just then. Perhaps that's why Zaki never made an attempt to kiss me on the lips. He's setting limitations to ascertain we didn't cross the boundaries of what was permitted at this point in our relationship. I felt warm inside. I suddenly experienced an urge to hug him right then.

"Perhaps he wants to do that on your wedding day, girl," Roshie said giggling. I noticed my temperature rose and heated my cheeks.

"By the way, what did he say about your vacation in England? He seems moody these days." Kaycee was always quick to notice these changes in people's behavior around the office.

"Yeah, he seemed troubled about it. But after the talk last night, I think we're good. He's just worried about what my brother will say. This has been going on for years now, and neither of them has met him, and we've not made any proper announcement."

"Okay. So now, what's your status?" They were all quiet after Joan asked the dreaded question, waiting for my answer.

"We are together," I said simply.

"What does that mean? We know you are together. It's been three years, Hanna. Everybody here knows that there is something between the two of you. But are you boyfriend and girlfriend, engaged, committed partners? That should be cleared, I think." Kaycee was not only sensitive to people; she was also sharp with her opinions.

"He asked me last night if I could live with someone like him. I said yes. And he said I would not regret it. That's it."

"OMG!! Really? Maybe he's going to propose soon!" Roshie's overexcitement was rubbing off on all of us. I felt my cheeks turning more crimson.

"Let's not get ahead of ourselves. For now, we've defined the direction of where we want this relationship to go. I'm happy about that, and relieved, I should add."

I had never been with any man for longer than two years. I must admit, I was starting to get alarmed about our relationship. The lack of a formal agreement, given that he was almost always away on business trips the past few years, or if he was around, there was his team to attend to and meetings to conduct, would have been understandable if I had given up. But there was something so beautiful about what we had that I could not see beyond myself alone. It was like finding something you had been wanting for all your life and finally being given it. I could not let go. I had held on to poor choices in the past. It was not that difficult to stay firm about something as amazing as our love.

The remaining week before my trip to England passed in relative peace, with me absorbed in finishing reports and ensuring that the needs of the team were well in place. Zaki and I had dinner on the night of my flight. He's sporting a somber face again. I reached for his hand across the table.

"Hey. What's with the serious face?" I was caressing his hand.

"What if your brother asks you to give me up?" That was totally unexpected for me. I was dumbstruck. It took me some time to react.

"Why would you think something like that?" I nearly choked on my response, my own words getting tangled with my tongue, so to speak.

"I'm a Muslim, Hanna. With all that's happening now and some of my Muslim brothers causing all those tragedies across Europe, it's not unthinkable for your brother or his family to think differently of me. Everyone is being too critical of us nowadays."

My heart felt the sadness of his every word in that expressed sentiment. I tightened my hold on his hand.

"My family is different. My brothers are different. They're both well-educated and have open minds. You need not worry about them having any untoward thoughts about Muslims or about you. Please don't worry yourself needlessly."

"I'm trying, but I'm failing. I feel as though this trip of yours to the UK will bring about changes for us which we both can't do anything about. I'm already shaking at the mere thought." He lowered his glance, probably so I would not see his eyes and the horror that he was feeling, that was growing by the minute. I moved to his side and took him into my arms.

He lowered his head to the level of my face, and I planted kisses on it. If I could fit him inside my heart then, I would. I would do anything to protect this beautiful man and our beautiful love.

"I'm sorry I'm being like this, with you hours away from leaving. Don't think I'm trying to stop you from going. I'm just saying that I can sense that this visit to your brother there will shift things for us. How? I don't know. I just feel that way."

"I understand you, though not what you're saying. I'm trying to determine the possible cause of this fear, the root from which this is connected. But I can't see beyond our current situation, to be frank. But please be assured that nothing will change, not with me, not with my feelings." I kissed his cheek and let my lips stay there, close to his.

He looked at me with those beautiful green eyes glowing with love for me. It's pure magic. How amazing that with a mere look, one could communicate feelings so deeply that would render words useless. I've never had love like this. I couldn't let this go. I couldn't let him go.

*

"Send me a message the soonest you reach there." There could be no other place safer than Zaki's arms. I didn't want to get out of it. "Hanna." I pulled away slightly and looked up at him.

"Be good while I'm away." I winked playfully at him.

"Always." He granted me a kiss on the forehead after another tight hug. "Now go before I whisk you inside the car again and drive off." It made me giggle.

"Oh, don't forget that we have a three-hour time difference. So, I might not be able to answer you right away, in case your message comes in too early for me."

"Noted, mademoiselle."

I gave him a flying kiss and walked into the airport.

*

My excitement was mounting the moment I reached the boarding lounge. *England! Wow!* It sure was a grand dream. After a magical experience in Egypt just eight weeks ago, there I was about to hop into a plane again to fly off to another dream destination. As I was looking at the photos of the touristic places to see in England, my phone vibrated with a message from my brother Henry.

Henry: I have duty tomorrow. Charisse will meet you at The airport. You'll both take the intercity bus heading for Coventry. I'll just see you at home in the early evening.
Me: Okay, Kuya. See you.

Half an hour after taking off, we encountered a turbulence and I was awakened because of it. The captain's voice could be heard throughout the cabin, reminding everyone to put on their seatbelts. I always had mine on, so I ignored the clamor in and outside the plane. I tried to sleep again. But we were shaking like crazy inside! I immediately thought of praying. Afterward, I imagined being with Zaki, his arms protectively wrapped around me. I managed to doze off again. The next thing I knew, our meals were being served.

With just two hours to go before we landed, my thoughts drifted back to the conversation we had over dinner. I had never seen Zaki that anxious before. I was still as clueless as to where it might have stemmed from. But the look on his face gave me the chills. He sure was dead serious about it. And so was my brother with his invitation. They were two different points from two separate lines, but somehow for Zaki, they were interconnected. Only I couldn't see it then just yet.

*

The British had very efficient system, and it didn't take me long to go through the entire process of Immigration. My luggage came out fast enough, too. There was free Wi-Fi and the signal was strong. I opened my phone and sent my niece Charisse a buzz in Messenger. We were jumping like long-lost teenage classmates when she arrived.

The bus ride home to Coventry was smooth. I had napped again. A moving vehicle always lulls me to sleep. Another short taxi ride from the station, and we're finally home. My little niece and nephew were playing on their front lawn. I dashed out to them with open arms. My sister-in-law came out to greet me. She's very welcoming, as always. But I caught something in her eyes that, in an instant, concerned me. It caused my heart to triple-beat per second. I had a long flight plus two hours of land travel. I was certain I wasn't imagining what I saw, but I didn't have the energy to deal with it yet. Tomorrow would be another day. I would be staying for two weeks, so I would have time – if it would turn out to be a matter that would really require attention or more so action.

I was suffering from a nasty cold for the first two days. My body wasn't liking the coldness of England. Though it's summer, it's still relatively cold, especially at night – for me at least, with my body more accustomed to the heat of Dubai.

Our first outings were just within Coventry. My sister-in-law took me and the kids to their local car museum and the mall. I shared some photos with Zaki on WhatsApp. I could tell that he had not relaxed a bit, but he seemed determined not to ruin my time here by being positive with his responses. I loved him more by the minute for doing so. My brother had not said anything yet as well if there was anything to be said at all. So, as I was closing in on my first week there, I was beginning to think that perhaps it was just some kind of paranoia on the part of Zaki to worry.

On Saturday evening, after our day out at Stratford-upon-Avon, the world-renown playwright William Shakespeare's hometown, I was heading to the kitchen to get some water when I overheard my sister-in-law asking my brother when he was going to talk to me. There was a door that separated the kitchen from the rest of the house. It was kept ajar at that time, so they didn't see or hear me approaching.

"She still has a week to be here. If you talk to her now, she still has ample time to mull over the matter. At least when she goes back to Dubai, she should be somewhat alright, with the matter having settled in her mind." There was genuine concern in my sister-in-law's voice.

What could this matter be about?

I quietly hurried back to my nephew's room upstairs and shut the door gently. My heart was beating so fast that I had to literally talk myself to calm down.

What could they want to talk to me about? My head was screaming Zaki's name. *But why? What about him?*

I picked up my phone and checked the time. It's just about ten in the evening. It's dinner time in Dubai. I thought of sending Zaki a message but had to stop, realizing I had no idea what to tell him. I tried lying down on the bed, but the rapid rise and fall of my chest made me uncomfortable. I felt like my intestines were interlacing, and I was starting to feel a knot in my stomach. I was pacing in the room, starting to sweat, though there was a cool breeze coming through the window.

They don't like Zaki for me? But they don't even know him. It's not fair!

The voice in my head was screaming, repeating words of protest louder and louder until it drove me to the edge of the bed. Finding myself kneeling beside it, I started to pray.

Father, I was never selfish in my wishes, never had been materialistic in my petitions. I never asked for more than what I believed I deserved. I have been good, Father. Please… I have always asked for just one man. Just one… Please let me keep him. Let me keep Zaki.

My body was uncontrollably shaking as tears drenched my face. I didn't know yet what they wanted to talk to me about, but my hunch alone was causing me unbelievable pain. Perhaps Zaki's right after all. The urge to message him was so strong. But I had to restrain myself for now since I didn't have actual data to base my conclusions on. Even when it seemed to be growing clearer to me by the minute that it was him they wanted to talk to me about, I must give them the benefit of the doubt. Sometimes when we act prematurely about a situation, it becomes muddier. I thought to myself that maybe they just wanted to know the real status of our relationship. Maybe my brother just wanted to get a better understanding as to where we were headed.

But why would they want me to have the time to think the matter over before returning to Dubai?

It must be something tremendously serious with the potential to affect my concentration at work.

I crawled onto the bed. I pulled the duvet right up to my face. I wanted to cover myself entirely from whatever was coming my way tomorrow or the day after. I thought of Zaki. I imagined myself in his arms, enveloped in his scent and warmth. I was close to falling asleep when I felt my phone vibrate underneath me. With one eye open, I checked who the message was from. *Zaki.* I lied on my back and opened the message.

> **Zaki**: I just had a run on the treadmill. I can't keep still. I don't understand why. You know how it is when a storm is about to come? People are rattled in anticipation.

I cried again. He sensed my current condition. My thoughts had reached him. The amazing power of love was at work here. Two people on either side of the world, anticipating the coming of the same storm, both growing restless and wishing for the other.

Me: I wish you were here with me right now. I could use a hug.

His response was immediate. The phone was in his hand, probably awaiting eagerly to hear from me.

Zaki: Hanna, what happened?

There was no point in keeping it from Zaki. He had the right to know. Even if I wasn't sure yet, there's a very good chance that the talk would be about him or concerning him.

Me: I overheard my sister-in-law telling my brother not to Delay talking to me. I didn't get to hear what it was about. But I didn't like the tone of her voice. She sounded gravely serious.
Zaki: Has your brother said anything to you so far?
Me: Nothing at all. In the last two days, he had been driving me around. Today we had an enjoyable time in Shakespeare's hometown. We rented a small boat, and my brother wheeled it from both ends of the river. Nothing. And I didn't sense anything from him either.
Me: On the way home, we planned my overnight stay in London tomorrow with his eldest daughter. All the talks we've had so far were just about the places I have yet to see.
Zaki: Have you spoken to your other brother back in the Philippines? Had he said something or hinted at anything?
Me: No, my brother Hector didn't mention anything. He just wished me to enjoy my trip here. So did Mom.
Zaki: Your brother asked you to come shortly after our

trip to Egypt. Hanna, I think I have a lot to do with that talk that they want to have with you. This trip isn't just for you to see England.

His words gave me goosebumps. I literally shuddered. I knew now that he could be right. It took me awhile to respond. The tears were blurring my sight. I felt the tiny pieces of my heart slowly ebbing away at the edges.

Zaki: Hanna, I don't want to go ahead with things here. But should your brother ask you to stay away from me, know that I'll not take it against him, or you, if you wish to follow him. I care so much about you. But I can't fight this battle. We cannot win this.

I gave a silent howl. More tears came. I sat up because my overwhelming emotions were starting to choke me. I must respond, but I couldn't get my fingers to move or for my mind to concoct the words together. I just kept saying his name. After some time, when I regained my composure, I replied.

Me: I dreamed about you in the past. I'm with you now. I don't want to lose you in the future. I may not survive the pain.
Zaki: I had been drawn to you since day one, Hanna. You're aware of what I feel for you. I may not have been as vocal, but you can vouch for my sincerity. I want to keep you in my life. But our families are important people in our lives too.
Zaki: This is really very difficult, and I'll not deny that I'm very affected. But really, I don't know what I can do.

Me: There must be another way. Please, Zaki, don't give up too easily.
Zaki: I'm not giving up, Hanna. I'm with you to whatever end.

Tears were still in abundance, soaking the front of my jumper now. But his words were infusing me with strength. I felt it straightening my back, preparing it for whatever burden that was ahead.

Zaki: Sleep now, Hanna. I'm holding you in my heart.
Me: I'm clinging close, Zaki. I'm not going to let go.

*

I didn't know how I fell asleep or at what time. Today I woke with the same sting in my heart. It's so quiet. I wondered where the kids might be. They would usually wake me up or join me in bed for a morning cuddle. But everything seemed very still this morning. I turned to look at the door. It was still closed, no trace that either one of my little munchkins had tried to open it. I slowly stretched, oddly fearing I might shatter physically with how broken I felt inside.

They must be in the kitchen, having breakfast.

I searched for my phone. I panicked a little when I couldn't find it. It was my only physical tie to the man I loved when we were not together.

No!

I raised the duvet, frantically searching for it. I heard a tumble on the floor. I immediately grabbed it as if it was the most important thing in the world. I pressed open it upon seeing Zaki's name.

> **Zaki**: It was a hard night for me. I couldn't sleep. I couldn't remember the last time I cried. The thought of us being separated tears me up inside out.

I felt how raw his emotions were. I was just as torn. I was about to cry again when my little niece and nephew burst into the room. They showered me with kisses on the face. Their laughter soothed my aching heart.

"Good morning, my little loves!" I took them both in my arms, kissing their heads one after the other.

"Mommy told us to wake you up. We're going to eat now," said my good-looking nephew, Liam, as he tugged my hand to get out of bed.

"Okay, I'll follow. Let me just go to the loo first."

They rushed downstairs while I forced my feet to walk to the bathroom. I wasn't ready to face them, especially my brother, but the longer this would drag on, the longer my agony would last.

My brother Henry had always been very gentle with me. When I erred, he reprimanded me calmly. He was a steady, quiet force, guiding me along while I was growing up. I had never dreaded talking to him, for he was always objective, calm, and almost politically diplomatic. But right there and then, I was wishing I was somewhere else.

I was relieved not to see my brother at the dining table. A tired mind, troubled heart, and an empty stomach would have easily made me lose any battle.

"Good morning, Ate (older sister). Where is Kuya?"

"Good morning, Hanna. Your brother has a duty. He left already."

I was still in high school when my brother, Henry, became a nurse. The word *duty* has been around our household since. But that day, for some strange reason, the word stirred me.

I ate slowly while checking my feeds on Facebook. I was aware of my sister-in-law's eyes on me, but I pretended as though I wasn't.

"Hanna, did you cry yourself to sleep last night? Your eyes are smaller than usual, and your lids look swollen." I liked Helen since day one. I think she was meant to be part of our family. We didn't have any initial awkwardness right from the start.

"I heard you and Kuya talking in here last night. What is it that you want to talk to me about?"

"Zaki and you." The bell in my mind collapsed from the tower and gave out an immensely loud bang. Zaki's hunch was right all along. He wasn't just imagining anything.

"What about us?" My heart was beating so fast that, at that moment, it seemed to be the only organ I had in my body.

"Hanna, what's your relationship with that man?"

"We are together. We plan to be together for life." The assurance that came from that promise kind of infused some strength into my weakening state.

"He's a Muslim. Are you willing to convert to Islam?" Decades of dealing with hospital patients and their families during critical moments had prepared my sister-in-law well for talks like this. She's very composed, her tone very calm and calculated.

"We already agreed on this matter. It's alright for Zaki for me to remain a Christian, and I have relented to the fact that our children will be raised as Muslims." Helen was quiet. She seemed to be thinking my response through. I sat motionless, unable to determine how to move or how to be. She dismissed the kids after the last spoonful she fed to my niece.

"I know you love him, Hanna. I can see it in your eyes. And I believe that he loves you too. Your pictures together spoke of that respect and love you both have for each other." My tears started to fall in big drops. I couldn't keep my eyes open. The heaviness of what I felt inside forced my lids to close.

"We're just thinking of the future – your future specifically. You're a very intelligent woman. I know that you have a very good understanding of Islam and Muslims. But, my dear sister, written information about Islam is not the same as to what it is in actuality. It's going to be a 360-degree turn for you."

I had always understood that Islam was more than just a religion for Muslims. Their faith permeated every aspect of their lives. That's one of the reasons that enamored Zaki to me. His devotion to his faith was his direction in life. The honor he held for his religion was the very same honor that defined him as a man.

"Right now, you are both still young and very much in love. But five or ten years down into your marriage, do you think he would not sit you down to rediscuss the matter of conversion? When you have children, for sure, he would want to bring them to Mecca, as that is an important aspect of their faith. Do you think he would not miss his wife with him during that crucial exercise? And if it's not him who will insist on conversion, I'm certain his family would."

I remained quiet. Her words made me conjure scenes of the future in my mind. I didn't mind wearing an abaya and veiling myself if need be. I was sure that I'd do whatever would be necessary for us to make things work.

"Hanna, you can't completely love and honor your husband if you don't share his belief. No matter how deep your love goes for each other, there will always be that one thing that separates you from him, and that's his faith. A Muslim who is devout in his faith will never turn his back on his beliefs, even for his wife. Please reconsider your relationship with him."

There was finality in her tone. It seemed that I had no option, or wasn't supposed to have even one other, on this matter. My tears were like water from a broken dam, rushing out and blinding my eyes. I didn't notice Helen had moved from her seat and come to me until I felt her arm on my shoulders. I leaned on her. She cradled me in her arms. My body was shaking wildly. The pain was so indescribable that I could only express it through tears.

"I'm sorry, Hanna. We love you. We're only thinking of what is best for you. It hurts terribly now, but you'll be alright. Your heart will heal in time. You'll love again. You'll meet another great guy. Let this one go. He's not for you."

"He's not for me? Then why did God allow us to meet? Why did He allow us to fall in love?"

"It wasn't God, Hanna; it was you. You chose to love him. Fate is such a bad joker, as they say. You have a good heart, both of you. Yet still, fate chose to play its nasty trick on you both. But there's a lesson to be learned in every situation such as this. If you look deep enough, you'll see what it is."

None of her words was making its way into my logic. I was feeling numb from scalp to sole. The beating of my heart was electrified with pain. If I had been cut open at that moment and each minute part of me was observed through a microscope, one would have seen how pain had penetrated every molecule of my body. I couldn't recall ever feeling such pain in my life prior. How could you let go of the one person you had been waiting for all your life?

*

It was five in the afternoon, and I was still in bed. The whole day, I was falling in and out of sleep, delirious. The vibration of my phone registered with me during sleep, but I couldn't make myself wake up to check it. When I finally did, I saw that Zaki had sent me a few messages on WhatsApp.

Me: I just woke up. I fell asleep crying this morning. Helen and I had the talk already. Zaki, they want us to separate.

He had read my message but no response. A full 15 minutes passed and I thought to myself, *He must be thinking of what to say back to me, or worse…what?!* The thought of Zaki probably crying felt like as though a boa constrictor was squeezing my heart. I have had boyfriends in the past who were probably hurt when we parted ways. But I couldn't recall ever concerning myself about them after the breakup. I had always channeled my energy into licking my own wound as I moved on. This time, it's different. I didn't want to part ways with Zaki. I hadn't thought of that. I didn't want to move on from him or without him. Life wouldn't be the same. I had waited for this kind of love. I had dreamed of this kind of man. I had prayed for him and been faithful in keeping myself together for someone like him. There should be a way to work this out.

Soft knocks on the door halted my thoughts. It was Sinead, my pretty little niece. She was peeking through the door and talking to her older brother.

"Come in here, both of you."

They joined me on the bed. Their movements seemed tentative and calculating like they were worried that approaching me would break me even more. I had to cajole them into my arms.

"We heard you crying earlier." Sinead's only four years old, still very much a baby, and yet she sounded like a mature kid having said that.

"Are you sad, Tita (aunt)?" Liam's handsome face displayed worry. He's only six.

I felt like crying again. I was always at my most sensitive when with my family, knowing too well that they wouldn't laugh at me if I displayed my vulnerability.

"Yes, I'm sad, Liam. But I'll be okay." I kissed his hair.

"But why are you sad?" His curiosity seemed genuine.

"I'm going to lose the man I love the most." I forgot I was talking to children. That just came out of my mouth.

"What do you mean?"

Death. It would mean death.

I'd further confuse them had I said that out loud. Sinead would grow up and would have a man in her life too. It seemed like a struggle to explain it, but it would be a disrespect not to try in any way that their baby minds could understand. I opened my phone and showed them a picture of Zaki.

"I love this man. His name is Zaki. But we can't be together anymore. Your dad doesn't like him."

"Our dad?" Liam's tone couldn't hide his disbelief.

"Yes, your dad, my Kuya Henry."

"But why? Does Dad know him?" I wished he did, for I was certain he would fall in love with Zaki's good character as well.

"No, they haven't met."

"So why is it that Daddy does not like him? Is he a bad guy?"

"No, princess, he's not a bad guy. He's a kind man. But our parents, our mom and dad, know what's best for us. So sometimes they'd ask us to part ways with some people."

I felt a tug in my heart after having said that. My brother Henry, just like our older brother Hector, had been a very hands-on brother, attentive, patient, and supportive. There was never a moment in my life growing up when either of them had ever been out of my sight or by my side. They're both the epitome of what a gentleman should be. Looking at my niece and nephew, I realized I had been blessed to have such brothers. Before any man, they and Dad were my first love. I had never gone against their wishes before. It dawned on me at that moment that I never could, no matter how old I became, out of my deep love and respect for both of them.

"What are you going to do, Tita Hanna?"

"I'll do as your dad asks, Liam. We should always listen to our parents. You both should always follow your mom, dad, and Ate Charisse. We are family. That's what being a family is about. We stay together, no matter what."

I couldn't stop the tears anymore. I allowed it to kiss my cheeks once again. The kids were just looking at me. Just then, my brother pulled up on the front lawn. They rushed down to meet their dad. I was looking at them from the window in Liam's bedroom. My brother opened his arms to take in his little angels. I imagined Zaki doing the same to our kids, and I would be at the door waiting. More tears came. When it's the heart crying, there's no stopping the tears at all. I lied down again, still crying, my sadness slowly swallowing me whole.

I heard my brother's voice from behind the door. I sat up, and he joined me on the bed. He reached out and touched my cheeks, wiping the tears with his thumb. I inched myself closer to him, and he took me in his arms. I missed being the little girl to the big brother that he was. There's always something so special about being in the arms of my brothers. I felt so safe and loved.

"The kind of future you're going to have is dependent on the choices you make today. It's painful, I know. But it's better you cry now than suffer later. I know he's a good guy. I know your taste. I helped raise you, Hanna. I know you. But I don't think you're fully aware of what you're actually getting yourself into once you're married to this man. Having said that, I don't mean to look down on him. But he's a Muslim man, not just any man. Muslims live by a code that centers on their faith. Unless you convert, and there's a high chance that at some point in your marriage that he might ask you to, you'll never really be completely a part of him by remaining a Christian."

His wife had pointed out the same thing that morning. Throughout the day, though I was slipping in and out of consciousness, I mulled over that matter. Despite the pain fogging my mind, I understood what they were telling me, and I believed them. It's just that it was so hard for my heart to embrace the thought. How could you make your heart listen to something that it didn't want to hear? How could you make your heart understand the very thing that's breaking it?

"I'll ask Helen to prepare dinner. Fix yourself and join us shortly. She told me you had been holed up in here the whole day. London missed you today. Don't let this matter make you miss the rest of what England can show you." He kissed me on the head and left the room. I stayed immobile for some time more. I was at a crossroads between familial duty and personal happiness. Either choice I made I was bound to break hearts, mine included.

*

"Tomorrow morning, I will drop you off at the bus station that will take you to London. Charisse will meet you there. I found a nice hotel close to the theater. I already booked you two for an overnight stay. In the evening, you both will go see The Phantom of the Opera at Her Majesty's Theatre. Charisse knows London very well. She'll be your guide."

That offered a respite to my aching heart. It wasn't what I wanted, but it was the only door opened for me.

"We will come pick you up on Tuesday. Then we'll go to Windsor Castle." I just nodded in affirmation.

"Hanna, a broken heart is not a tragedy. It's a lesson. It may be very hard now, but you'll soon realize it gets easier with time. Grieve but don't stop living." My brother's words moistened my eyes. I had been crying in the last 24 hours for more than I could remember, and yet there seemed to be no end to my tears.

I packed light for my overnight trip to London. I sent a message to my niece, Charisse, about our itinerary. After checking in at the hotel, she'd take me to two museums, and we'd have a walk around the city proper afterward. At seven in the evening, we'd go to the opera.

The National History Museum was a fantastic place to lose oneself. However, my interest inclined heavier toward human history and the remains they left us, so it was the visit to the British Museum that pleased me more.

Animals could outlive us twice over. A tortoise on display at the National History Museum died at two hundred years old. But it was man's history that lasts longer because of our capacity to leave marks of our existence. For this very reason, the past made itself so fascinating to me. The British Museum held within its walls some of the most beautiful creations of man from the world over. Of course, what held my attention more than anything was those taken from Egypt, the Rosetta Stone in particular. The remains of the earliest Persian and Indian civilizations rival those of ancient Egypt. But neither one could challenge my love for the latter, especially with Zaki now adding weight to that desire. Every part of me was wishing for him with every minute that passed. Great civilizations made history. But what of great loves? How could the world be reminded of the great battles fought inside the heart?

My niece was busy taking photos when I saw the notice for the ongoing show on recovered artifacts from the sea in

Alexandria. My heart instantly lifted at the decision. But I hesitated just as fast. In the state I was in, I was sure I would not be able to hold my attention right, nor prevent my emotions from littering the place. There would be another chance for it. Right now, I wanted some natural air and light. I started to feel boxed in.

"Charisse, when you're done here, just follow me outside. I'd be right by the door. I need some air."

"We can go now, Tita Hanna."

She didn't ask if I was alright. I was sure my distress was visible. My facial blood vessels had the propensity to turn my cheeks red when I was aroused with emotions, be it for happy or sad reasons.

The light outside was refreshing. It's just five in the afternoon. The sun's rays here were not as harsh as in the Middle East.

"Do you want to see the famous London Eye, Tita Hanna? We have enough time before the show tonight."

"Sure." The tour of London wouldn't be complete without seeing it and the Big Ben, I supposed. Upon reaching there, however, it was the River Thames that caught my eyes more than anything. So much of history and life had changed around it, but there it was, still as majestic as ever. After a few photos, we went about our way. Charisse was an excellent guide. She knew the alleys and streets to take in order to get to any destination. The next thing I knew, we were on a hop-on, hop-off double-decker bus and rounding the city. I allowed myself to be entertained by the beautiful rows of houses and churches we passed on, side by side with modern shops. History and modernization collided smoothly.

The performance at the opera transported me to another time. It managed to make me set aside all thoughts of Zaki. But when the actors sang the main theme song, my emotions were stirred once more, making me tear up quietly in the dark.

No more talk of darkness. Forget these wide-eyed fears… When will my freedom from this come?

The performance closed with a standing ovation. I wouldn't be walking out of my own story as a victor, though. No one would applaud the extraordinary sacrifice our hearts would be making in the name of faith and for the sake of family.

My niece asked if I was hungry. She pulled me out of my head. I hadn't eaten enough in the last few days. I thought it would be good to fill me up then. We stopped by at a local restaurant near our hotel. I cleared a big plate of rice and baby back ribs.

"Are you feeling better, Tita?" Charisse had been very respectful of my silence since that morning. At such a young age, she's showing an extraordinary virtue in sensitivity.

"Yes. This place is awesome. I loved the food. Do you want anything else?" I eyed the fries overflowing off the bowl at another table. "Maybe we can have a serving of that too?"

"Your appetite's back!" It was a funny comment to make, and I smiled curtly at her.

"So, I'd take that as a yes." I nodded for a waiter to come over. Not long after, our new orders came. We spoke of trivial things, her schooling and a part-time job. She didn't dare ask about Zaki, and neither did I volunteer to bring him up.

It was a difficult walk back to the hotel, though it was a mere five minutes distance, what with our filled bellies.

"Thank you for today, my love. I enjoyed it." I hugged her and kissed her forehead when we reached the foyer of the hotel.

"You're welcome, Tita. It's a small matter, but I hope today's outings helped in any way."

"It did, yes. London is busy, but it's beautiful. And you seem to know it very well."

"I have been living here for two years now. When I turned 18, Mom and Dad allowed me to leave out, and I chose London."

"Good choice."

"Tomorrow they and the kids will be here by 11 in the morning. They'll take you to Windsor Castle. You'll like it there."

"I'm looking forward to it."

The full meal helped bring in sleep. I fell asleep shortly after arriving back. I had a dream, a bizarre sequence of events, and in one scene I saw Zaki walking into a mosque. There were people, all strangers to me, walking about and minding themselves. I looked to my right, and I saw the faint silhouette of the pyramids under the setting sun. I looked at Zaki again, and he was slowly disappearing into the mosque. I wanted to call him, but I couldn't find my voice. I stared at his figure until he completely ceased to be visible from my sight.

I woke up breathing heavily. I stood and quietly walked to the window. The sun would be rising shortly, the very tip of it was already starting to emerge from the horizon. A new day was dawning. *Let daylight dry your tears...* The song humming softly inside me again. *Zaki*... Tears once more came.

Father, my heart is in pieces. Please, keep the rest of me together. Help me make it through another day.

After a hearty lunch at the same restaurant Charisse and I dined at last night, my brother took the road that would take us to Windsor Castle. I was quiet on the way. I really had nothing to say. All were decided for us so nothing left for me to do but accept it completely and act upon the decision made for me.

"How are you?"

"I'll live."

"You must. The way forward is your only option, or should I say, the only logical option." I stayed quiet. To argue was futile, and I had no strength left for it.

"Hanna, I hope you don't hate me or us for this. Be angry if you must, but don't hate us for this."

"I don't hate you, Kuya." I couldn't put as much emotion into my words. I was really feeling spent.

London was just a short distance from the Windsor Castle. I put a firm grip on my emotions and determined to use my strong mind to direct my actions once more. I've always wanted to see and be in a castle. I was walking toward one now. I wanted to be fully immersed in the experience.

Even from the outside, what could be seen of the castle was an imposing sight. Gift shops lined the street leading to its entrance. Once I set foot within it, I was filled with excitement.

Another dream came true.

When fully inside its grounds, I allowed myself to daydream. The entire complex was huge. The lawns were manicured, the courtyards were very clean, and the castle itself didn't display its age or its deep and long history. It looked so strong and poised despite the passing of time. According to the booklet I bought from the shop inside, the castle had gone through many changes with each monarch who used it during their reign. Some years back, it survived a catastrophic fire. Looking at the castle from the outside, it was hard for me to reconcile that. It's indeed worthy to be called a fortress.

The interior was expectedly splendid. The grandeur from every corner could easily make any lady feel like a princess or even a queen. However, I wasn't as impressed. My eyes were entertained, but I was no fan of extravagance. The place made me feel insecure, what with the halls and towering portraits gilded in gold frames. I felt like it held more importance than me, that if someone were to visit me, the grandness of the castle interiors would hold my guest's attention more than I would.

There were two sections in the castle that redeemed it to my taste, however – the Grand Vestibule, where the collections of arms and swords of King George IV were kept, and the St. George's Hall, where the ceilings displayed the coats of arms of England's former knights and by its walls the armors. England's history of chivalric knights and swordsmen never failed to regale me.

We rested for some time on the grass grounds, just right outside the long procession road where the queen's entourage normally passed. The afternoon temperature had a sweet, romantic note to it. I lay down on the cold grass and looked at the sky. It's a beautiful day, no indication of rain. However, the storm inside my heart hadn't subsided, nor was it showing any signs of stopping any time soon.

The drive back to Coventry was pleasant. I liked the trees lining both sides of the highways. I fell asleep halfway through. The horn from a truck awakened me, but I kept my eyes closed.

"She seems okay now. Perhaps the trip to London helped," I heard what my sister-in-law said.

"She has no choice but to be okay and be better. Hanna has a resilient spirit. She'll pull through. It may take time, but she'll be alright."

Will I ever be alright? Will I ever be able to recover from this?

I dozed off for the remainder of the drive. It was my nephew, Liam, who woke me up upon reaching home. I went straight to his room and fell asleep. I woke up from the breeze coming through the opened window. It was almost nine in the evening. There were messages from Zaki waiting for me to read. I felt hollow. I closed my eyes again. The next moment I opened them again, it was three in the morning.

Me: I was tired from the excursions I had with my family yesterday. I'm sorry for my late response. I'm okay and enjoying my time here. How are you?

I wasn't expecting any response from him given how late it was, but my phone vibrated as I was to get off the bed for the toilet.

Zaki: I'm okay. I'm missing you a lot. I'm in Saudi right now. I had meetings here today. I'm going back to Dubai tomorrow.
Me: Let me know when you've reached home, please.
Zaki: Yes, I will. Go back to sleep. I'm holding you in my heart.
Me: And you're in mine too.

*

Soft knocks on the door pulled me out of sleep. It's Charisse. It's 11 in the morning!

"Hi, Tita. Sorry to wake you up. But it's almost lunch. We're going to Birmingham. Dad asked me to wake you up."

"Okay. I'll go shower now."

The family of my brother's friend joined us for lunch. The couple seemed like a lovely pair. They're both from our country.

Did my brother invite them to show me how easy it is to be with our own people?

I felt my phone vibrate inside my shoulder bag. Zaki sent me a message.

Zaki: I hope you managed to fall back to sleep again. I'm heading to the airport for my flight back to Dubai.
Me: Yes, I did, and it stretched till 11, actually! We're in

Birmingham now, another city close to Coventry. We're in a mall having lunch with my brother's friends. Have a safe flight home. I miss you.
Zaki: Same here, every day.

I felt emotional, but I reminded myself that I was in public. I closed my eyes and uttered a simple prayer.

Father, please keep my heart in your hands. Help me stay together.

When I raised my gaze, my brother was looking at me. I nodded at him to affirm that I was alright.

We walked around the mall. This was the least thing I liked to do when outside. I saw a bookstore and told my brother to come back for me there. This was my other paradise, the first one being the beach.

There were a few I thought were worth buying, but I had to settle for just one. I chose *The Art of War, The Ancient Classic.* I had always been drawn to leadership books, especially if they had any historical background. There's a stool in the corner. I sat there and started to read while waiting for my family to come back for me.

It's an interesting read. I was well into the first 20 pages when I heard knocks on the window of the shop. It was my nephew, Liam.

"Tita, we're going to Wimbledon!" He seemed excited.
"Do you like tennis, Liam?"
"Yes. I like to watch."
"Will there be any matches today?"
"I don't know."

The drive would be nearly three hours, according to my brother. Good thing I bought a book; it would help me not mind the distance and could take my attention off my emotions.

Sun Tzu's teachings to win the war were strategic and displayed his deep intelligence. I wondered how Zaki and I could use his lessons to win the war of ideas and opinions with our families. I had studied the religions of the world, and not one I could recall where its founder meant to cause division amongst people. However, the followers themselves, bored and malcontent, created the rifts that now cast the world down to the roads of chaos and misunderstandings. I wanted to hate all of them who had started the clash between Christians and Muslims. All of what they had done had predestined this calamity that now befell Zaki and me. My temperature started to rise. I felt my cheeks heating up.

> **Me:** Do you think if we met in the past when our world's History was just starting, we had a better chance?
> **Zaki:** I can't say I have ever contemplated that thought. Your mind seems to be on to something. What is it, Hanna?
> **Me:** I'm just wondering, as usual. It seems to be the only Thing I'm free to do these days. My mind seems to be the only place where I can be free.
> **Zaki:** Did something happen, Hanna?
> **Me:** It's all inside my heart, Zaki. On the outside, all is well.

He left me to my thoughts. Not long after, sleep took me out of this world and into the land of mysteries and fantastical anomalies.

I opened my eyes, and all I could see was what was ahead of me. I had to turn my entire head in order to see what was on my left or on the right. I felt constricted in my movements, and it seemed that I made sounds with each turn. My hands felt heavy too. I looked down and saw a sword in my right hand and a shield in my left. I was fully armored! There was faint thundering noise from a distance in front of me.

Where am I? What's going on?

Then I heard a voice.

"Hanna! Concentrate! Focus your mind! Ahead of you is either freedom or death. Keep your mind on your sword and your shield, nothing more. Do you understand?"

How could I understand any of this? How could I be here?

"Hanna! Hanna!" The stranger removed his helmet and disclosed to me his identity.

"Dad?"

"Hanna, there's a big battle ahead. Focus on your strength, my love. Your life is in your hands. If you die or live is all a matter of your choosing."

"Dad!"

I felt a hand on my arm. I woke up very alarmed. My brother was standing beside me. We've stopped. We're parked at a gasoline station.

"What were you dreaming about? You're calling Dad."

"He spoke to me in my dream. He said there was a battle ahead and that I must focus on my strength. If I live or die is up to me." My chest was still rapidly going up and down as I retold my brother my dream.

"What we've spoken about at home is just the beginning of your emotional battle. There's still much that lies ahead. Dad is right – focus on your strength. There's nothing else to be done, Hanna, but to let go. And I hope that when time presents you with that choice, you will choose accordingly."

I felt the weight of my brother's words. I had decided that I would do as they had asked, but he seemed to sense my hesitation.

"There's a washroom at the back of the store. Go freshen up. After ten more minutes, we will recommence on our trip."

The cold water on my face was refreshing. I wish I could also wash my heart to rid it of the emotions that were making it greasy. The dream had me reeling. So, it was right, as had been said. Some of the greatest battles that would be fought in this world would not be seen by the eyes but would be felt by the heart.

"Focus on my strength," I repeated my father's words to me.

The Wimbledon Arena was closed, but the tour for visitors was ongoing. It was drizzling, making the air colder. But the dream raised my temperature.

The Wimbledon Lawn Tennis Museum housed a good collection of paraphernalia donated by champions. It also showcased the evolution of the game through the years, from how the racket had been improved to how it looked like now. It was an entertaining visit for me.

*

I was looking at the gray skies while lying on the bed when my brother knocked on the door.

"Good morning, Hanna. We're going to Liverpool today. There's an important museum you need to see. Come on, let's eat now."

The museum was that of The Beatles. It was a must-see indeed. John Lennon's original white piano was on display there. On the wall were the lyrics of his song "Imagine." My heart got agitated again. My internal jukebox started playing the song even without me queuing for it.

Imagine there are no countries. It isn't hard to do. Nothing to kill or die for, and no religion too.

That was a hard hit. I stood still and closed my eyes to steady myself.

Imagination is for the idle. Reality is imagination that has come to life. But you must live in order to make that happen. The wise words from our father when I told him, at seven years old, that I would travel to Egypt to see the pyramids once I grew up. It troubled me that I seemed to trouble him from the other side of the veil. I wondered if Zaki's father had visited him in his dream the way mine had.

On the way to another castle, my brother passed by the strawberry fields that were mentioned in one of the famous songs of The Beatles. There were no strawberries, but only wild grasses confined in a walled area with a red gate.

The castle he wished us to visit was closed, so we proceeded to Kensington Palace instead. We roamed the grounds for some time. There's a regal statue of Queen Victoria in the middle of a pond.

How does a woman become a queen?

Even the rock replica of that once great monarch spoke of strength and poise that I could only wish for myself.

We walked further. The kids were happily running around, chasing squirrels, at Hyde Park. I saw a white swan in the lake, serenely floating in the water, poised in its stead. I recalled the story of the ugly duckling I read so many times while I was young. That swan was once a duckling, weak and uncertain, puddling clumsily in the water. Life and time turned it into that confident swan, afraid of the water no more.

That's how one becomes a queen.

There was no army for me to command, only emotions to master and to stay firm in mind. The swan's feet may be wading rigorously underneath the water, but its outward demeanor does not display that.

The grace of a swan and the strength of a queen. What a daunting undertaking!

I looked up at the sky. The clouds were parting faster, and rain seemed inevitable.

We continued our walk leading to the Albert Memorial Hall. We couldn't stay longer, though. Rain was approaching.

"We must go to the Albert Memorial Hall now before the rain pours. That's the closest we can run for shelter."

The kids were running ahead of us. They had been born here, and they're running as though their feet had always known the land, and the land in return guided their feet. I wished for some natural force to come to my aid then. Inside, I was tattering as the days went by. How long I could fake my strength, only God knew. I was longing for Zaki's arms more and more each day.

The rain was short. After a stroll inside, we resumed walking back to where my brother had parked.

"I think it's best we head home now. The rain might come again." I just nodded in affirmation.

The drive back home was quiet. I fell asleep so did the kids. When I awoke, my brother had just entered their garage. I offered to carry Sinead inside. She's still asleep.

*

I was watching a documentary on YouTube when I got a notification in Messenger. It was from my brother Hector.

Hector: Hi Hanna. How's your vacation so far? Mom is extending her regards.
Me: Hi Kuya. All's going as planned. We have been Visiting places around here. England is beautiful. You should come too.
Hector: I will. Let's have a reunion there, the three of us With Mom.
Me: That sounds really nice.

There was no reply after some minutes, so I resumed what I was watching.

Hector: Henry told me he had spoken to you about Zaki.
Me: Yup.
Hector: We're your family. Henry and I had been discussing this for some weeks before your trip there. We thought we shouldn't delay any longer. I thought it was just some infatuation you have for this guy. But your visit together in Egypt worried us deeply, Hanna. We knew we had to act.

I was quiet, processing my brother's message. Somehow, Zaki was right all along.

Hector: Hanna, my dear sister, please don't be mad. Or if You are, just be that. Don't hate us.
Me: I don't hate you, Kuya, or Kuya Henry. I understand. I'd do as you asked. Does Mom know?
Hector: She does. She worries for you.
Me: Tell her not to. I'll be fine.

I knew that was a lie. I knew it would take me some time to be fine again or maybe never, but I couldn't afford for our mother to worry that much at her age.

How did it come to this?

*

Four days more, and I would be going back to Dubai. My brother's vacation had been called off for the following two days. He's a theater nurse. He's needed to assist in emergency operations. I had no driver, so I thought there'd be no outings for me for two days. But then, as I was browsing through my feeds on Facebook, I saw a post from my friend's friend, whom I met in Abu Dhabi on one occasion. She's back in the UK. I sent her a message on Messenger.

> **Johanna:** Nice to hear from you, Hanna! Great that you're here. Where are you staying?
> **Me:** Coventry, with my brother and his family. Can we meet? I'm heading back to Dubai in four days.
> **Johanna:** Sure. I'm free today. But I'm in London. Do you know how to move around here on your own?
> **Me:** Well, not really. Do you mind meeting me at the bus Station in London? My brother can't drive for me. He's been called to the hospital to assist in some emergency. But I can take the bus.
> **Johanna:** Sure. What time do you think you can make it?
> **Me:** I'll leave now. It would take me a little over two hours. Shortly after 12 noon I guess I'd reach there.
> **Johanna:** Alright. Let's keep in touch, then.

"Ate, I'm going to London to meet a friend. How can I get a taxi to go to the bus station?"

"We can call for one. Who are you meeting there?"

"Johanna. She's an intern at the Abu Dhabi Falcon Hospital where my friend works. I met her there during one of my visits. We agreed to meet once I'm here. She'll meet me at the bus station."

"Are you sleeping over in London?"

"No. I'll come back tonight."

*

Johanna took me to the Victoria and Albert Museum. The collections it guarded were magnificent works of art. My eyes couldn't decide which to look at first! Sculptors created by genius hands survived hundreds of years to remind us now of our glorious past. There was no shortage of passion, talent, and intelligence in their craftsmanship. It was a mesmerizing two-hours stroll inside. Silently, I wished I could create something too that could tell the world of my immense love for Zaki.

"So, how are you enjoying England so far?"

"Yours is a beautiful country. I'm having a really good time. How have you been?"

"All good, though I'm tired a lot these days working on my papers."

"I wish you all the luck on that. And thanks for today. I appreciate you coming out to see me."

"It's good to see you too, Hanna. I'm glad for this short break to take my mind off school."

"Do you remember that guy we spoke about while I was there at Gregely's place?"

"The Muslim guy?" Muslims had names, but their religion seemed to be their single, foremost identifier amongst people. In my opinion, the media was to be blamed for this.

"Yes, him. Zaki."

"Oh yeah, Zaki. What about him?"

"My family asked me to separate with him."

"That sucks. But maybe that's for the better." Everybody in my circle seemed to think the same. Why couldn't I see the good in that decision?

"Why do you say that?"

"Hanna, we live in a very different time compared to that of our parents and grandparents. Politics had poisoned so many good things in this world, including love." Johanna was 12 years younger than I was, and yet her wisdom shamed mine. Perhaps it was time I gave considerable thought to their words.

"Life or death," I said softly while in contemplation on the bus ride home. That's what my father said in my dream. Surely my life would be very different without Zaki in it. But as Johanna said, politics has corrupted many things in our world. Could I allow it to take my chance to find another happiness?

Chapter 6

"Elope!" Lana's excited and slightly high pitch caught the attention of those from the nearby table. We had decided to snack at a coffee lounge after hours of scouring the shops in Ibn Battuta Mall.

"And go where?" My voice was mellow but serious.

"Anywhere! There are countries in the world where you can both live and not have to think about your religions."

From the corner of my eye, I saw the guys at the next table eyeing me questioningly. Lana's loudness invited for an unsolicited attention.

"Such as where?"

"Japan, Hong Kong, or Monaco. Turkey would be nice too. He can still practice his faith while you go to our own church."

I had to admit that Lana's idea did seem good – and very tempting. But my conscience couldn't agree to it completely. It would be like escaping, turning our backs on those we love.

"I'm excited at the prospect of starting a new life in another country where no one knows us. But it's something I'm not certain Zaki would agree to. And Lana, what about our families? No, we can't do that."

"They'll eventually come around to the idea, Hanna. They are your family. They will accept you back."

That may be true, but it seemed too much for our families to have to go through. And my brothers were two of the sweetest and most loving hearts in the world. I couldn't even bear to think that I'd hurt them in any way. My mom, too, was of advanced age. The thought that she might suffer a heart attack because of my selfishness was beyond me to even imagine. And what of Zaki's family? I couldn't begin to think how his mother and relatives would react. It would be a scandal. They could denounce him!

"There must be another way, girl." She was trying to console me, seeing how confused and hurt I was.

"Yes, there's a way – to separate. Perhaps we're not really meant for each other. There are people who love each other and yet they're not together, can't be together, shouldn't be to…" I choked on my own words, and tears gushed out of my eyes. I was aware that we were in public. I hardly cry in front of people, but the weight I was carrying inside was getting heavier by the day.

Lana rushed to my side and was rubbing me on the back. My body was uncontrollably shaking, and my heart felt like exploding. I had never known such pain. I felt like I was disintegrating little by little, and the air was taking away my tiny pieces to far-off destinations and would never allow me to be whole ever again.

"Why do your differing religions have to matter? You're in love. Why is that not enough?"

In the fantasy world of Disney or the movies, it should be enough. In reality, in the world of men and women and at a time when people differ from each other not just by races but also by beliefs, love wouldn't be enough. Love shouldn't be the only truth worth seeking and living; faith should be too. My mind, though it's a very hard truth to accept, understood the whole situation without much explanation required. It was my feelings I had to master.

"There are age-old traditions and beliefs that can't be bypassed because of love. Love is not the universal law – respect is," I surprised myself having said that. I felt the impact of my own words, momentarily offering a window for me to breathe in logic.

The two guys occupying the closest table to our left were quiet. I was sure they were listening to us, unexpectedly caught by the drama unfolding before them.

"If Zaki really loves you, he shouldn't force you to convert. He should accept you for what you are and respect what you believe in."

That's the prevalent argument of those who were in interfaith relationships here: that love should conquer all things and everyone. It sounded so romantic. For me, however, romance was not the only catalyst that could help a relationship survive. To disregard, or put aside at the least, one's religious belief was to settle for the temporal comforts that the relationship could give. Enjoy now and think later. It lacked the security I wanted and was a waste of time. For a woman to accept this was like setting the stage for mediocrity. And what kind of a man would one be if he were willing to ignore the very traditions and customs that made up his Muslim identity just so he could accommodate the adjustments demanded by his relationship with a non-Muslim? Indeed, the high road was not an easy path to walk on to. I would be gravely insulting Zaki if I asked him to leave that road and walked with me to the ways of the world. On the other hand, I would be mocking my own integrity as a Christian woman, willing to bend my beliefs in order to get my way. To choose between him and my family was a breaking point I never wanted to be at. My identity was my family. My dream was Zaki. What a torment!

It took me some time to prim myself. Lana asked the waitress for more tissues. A hand was extended to us from the neighboring table, and in it were folded pieces of tissues. I looked up at the guy and tried to smile at him awkwardly.

"Love is the source of both our ultimate joy and sorrow. To cry is a way of exhaling." I accepted the tissues and politely thanked him. I gently wiped my tears.

"I'm sorry to trouble you. It's not like me to cry before the world."

"The clouds never apologize when they pour rains, neither has the earth complained. You don't owe us an explanation for your tears."

"Thank you. That's very nice of you to say."

"You're welcome. My name is Mohammad. And this is my friend Ishmael."

"I'm Hanna. She's my friend Lana." They bridged the short gap and took our hands in theirs.

"Firm grip with soft hands. You're a passionate lady, my princess. Lucky is the man you love. There will be no shortage of affection for him."

"Only we cannot be together."

"So I heard. I don't mean to eavesdrop on your conversation. The distance between our tables is just a little over an arm's length."

"And we're talking a little too loudly." I gave a knowing look at Lana, who smiled sheepishly out of embarrassment.

"I married a Christian girl. We're divorced now. You're right. Love is not the answer to everything. I thought that marrying her was the greatest way I can show my love. I paid little thought to my religion, to the dismay of my family. May Allah forgive me for hurting them."

I felt a pull inside my heart. I didn't wish to see Zaki in the same situation. Shame followed my sadness, with no preamble or invitation, the emotion invaded me swiftly. I felt my cheeks heat up.

"Thank you for sharing your story with me. I appreciate your openness. May you find the love that's rightly yours and that it will stay." I held out my left hand to him. He took it and encased it with both of his.

"Thank you, princess. I pray the same for you. Religion is a very good thing, though many think it's the cause of today's problems." I shook my head to show my disagreement. "I don't think so, too. What would have become of us without it? Throughout history, the world over, religion was what kept communities of people together and survived the many obstacles of this life."

He's studying the outlines of nerves and lines on my hand. "I can't read palms, but I can tell that this hand wants to be held. Your slender fingers need to be kept within the muscular hand of a man who can understand your tenderness and respect your strength. May Allah give you the desires of your heart, princess. But if He cannot, may He grant you wisdom to understand why." Tears came easily again. I bowed my head in quiet contemplation of this stranger's words.

"It's hard to understand the ways of fate, but if we resist or fight it, it only muddles the water even more, as they say. Let him go. I'm not in the position to say that, or to say anything. But sometimes holding on or fighting life is not a display of love, rather an act of foolishness."

I felt the sincerity of his words through his hands, which were still enclosing mine. After a few more minutes, he released it, and I smiled at him through my tears.

"Thank you. It's very nice meeting you. Your words are adding clarity to my clouded judgment."

"You're welcome, Hanna. You'll heal in time. When you're ready again, God will let you meet the man for you."

Could one ever heal from this kind of devastation? He said in time. When is that? How, when every inch of me felt broken?

I bowed my head slightly when they bid us farewell. His unexpected kindness had offered me some relief. His words had lent some strength to my weakened resolve.

*

"Where are you?" Kaycee was waving at me across the dining table.

I was having lunch with my female colleagues. While in the middle of our exchanges, I suddenly fell quiet, my thoughts carrying me to some distant, unknown place. I muttered a simple apology.

"You need some distraction. There's a long weekend coming. Perhaps it can do you good to go somewhere," Kaycee suggested.

"Some of my friends are planning a trip to Jordan. You like ancient history, right? You may like it there. Check it out." Joan's suggestion lit me up from within.

The moment I got home, I checked Jordan on the internet. The pink city of an ancient civilization that had been lost to time, the Dead Sea, various historical places of interest with ruins, my wanderlust was growing as I checked each must-see site. I opened another page and checked the price of the tickets. It's reasonable enough. I checked for visa requirements and processing time. I had to apply right away so I could make it to the next local holiday.

Me: Ashley, I'm thinking of going to Jordan on the coming long weekend. Do you want to come with me?
Ashley: Yes, babe! Please plan it and let me know when We need to buy our tickets.

There's no escaping the pain that had fully occupied my heart and my being. So, I knew I needed to be more proactive to get better emotionally and mentally. Zaki was in France for work. We hadn't spoken since I came back from England – at least not *the* talk I was expecting. But our actuations toward each other hadn't changed. He hadn't changed. It's both comforting and saddening. At my most vulnerable, his arms remained my safe haven. But I was fully aware that at some point, sooner, I would need to end my dependency on its warmth and security. A tear escaped my closed lids and slid down my left cheek.

What would I be like after him?

Our flight was at seven in the morning. Terminal 2 was teeming with people. Instinctively, my eyes scouted the entire area, looking for a face. I hadn't seen Zaki for weeks on end. After he returned from the head office, he flew to Bahrain and then to Oman for meetings. It's as if fate was already starting on its plan to separate us. We were made to meet, and now the universe was doing a reverse course.

I knew I wouldn't find him here. But for some strange reason, I was hoping that some fragments of him would be here, having had to be in this terminal for so many times. I inhaled deeply, foolishly wishing to pick up his scent in the ventilated air. The longing I felt pierced me deep inside.

The flight was short, but it afforded me to nap. I had a dream. I was wearing an abaya and was properly veiled while standing on a carpet and my hands lay open, palms to the sky, and my lips were moving, but I felt empty in my heart. Then, all too suddenly, something was spilling out of my mouth. Letters! No, words! The words I was uttering in prayer were coming out of my mouth like vomit. I was choking, and I collapsed, open-eyed, before a darkening sky. I woke up shaking.

"Babe, are you alright?" Ashley was visibly alarmed.

"Yes. Was I saying anything or making any sound at all while asleep?"

"You were, but almost like a whisper, and your eyes were moving. I was wondering if I should wake you up."

"It was a disturbing dream. Bizarre."

"Was it about Zaki?"

"It's related to him, yes."

"Have you spoken to him?"

"No, we haven't had the chance. He's been on business trips almost in succession. And frankly speaking, I really don't know what else is there for us to talk about."

Our destiny had been decided. It wasn't a decision that favored either of us, but neither was it so bad considering that the happiness of our families were at stake.

"Is it not so difficult for you both, given that you work in the same company?"

"I have thought of resigning while I was in England. I thought it was a practical thing to do. But what is the practicality of losing the one you love?"

"Is there really no way for your families to compromise?"

"Zaki and his family are practicing, devout Muslims. For generations before him, both his parents were from Muslim families. He's the only son of his parents. He wouldn't break their tradition, neither would I make him, just for me."

"But what about both your happiness? I thought he loves you."

"He does. I believe he does. And he knows I love him too. But what will become of this love, of us, if we insist against the wills of our families? We can't be truly happy together knowing we have offended the very people we both love the most."

"This is giving me goosebumps, babe. Why does love have to be so complicated?"

Why indeed. But was it love that was complicated, or was it us, people, and the rules we had set? The captain's voice could be heard throughout the cabin, announcing our descent as we were closing in on our destination. I tried to think of what would be waiting for me to discover in Jordan as a way to divert my mind from the troubling dream.

Apart from the conveyor stopping for a good 15 minutes, our time inside the airport was a breeze, considering the number of tourists visiting Jordan at that time. After a short negotiation for our taxi ride to Petra, south of Jordan, we were on our way. The drive took nearly three hours. To a tourist, it would have been a boring desert ride. There's nothing much to see except sands and sporadic greens along the way. Ashley was sick due to the lack of air conditioning in the car and fell asleep. As a traveler, the ride for me was a journey toward a destination in a time when people lived in rocks and caves, a time that today's world deems as primitive. The landscapes on both sides of the roads were mostly flat and seemingly desolate. But the desert had its own allure. When I went on a Desert Safari tour with a colleague some time back, I noticed that the desert had its own beauty so unique to it. When one looked long enough at the mountains of sand created by the wind, one would see that it had a distinctive color – not dark yellow or dark brown as how it's commonly depicted in illustrations. It's almost golden when you take portions in your hand. The sand quality in this country was very fine too. And just like that, my mind drifted back to the time when I was standing on the boulders of the great pyramid of Khufu in Giza in Egypt. My heart started to race when my memory brought back the dream I had on the plane on the way back to Dubai.

What's with planes and these troubling dreams?

The camels we passed on the road cut through my thoughts. A young boy, probably just seven or eight, was mounted on one of them. He didn't seem scared at all. He must have been riding since he was a toddler to have that confidence to be on his own. Then a realization came to me.

That had been their life, and it will always be so.

Right. Bedouins remain Bedouins, regardless of how the world has changed and advanced. We're now into the millennia of time, and yet they remained in their own age, living their lives and their beliefs as they always had. My thoughts rushed Zaki into my consciousness. He's like the Bedouins in a way. He would always be a Muslim. Wherever in the world he would go, whatever he would choose to do, whoever he would choose to be with, he would always be and foremost a Muslim. The ache in my heart was tugging at my strength. I closed my eyes to stop the forthcoming tears. Suddenly, the screen in my mind displayed my burning image in front of the pyramid. I opened my eyes all at once, petrified of my own destruction. It may have been just a dream, but it had an impact so deep and troubling that I found myself crying to sleep the following nights after having it.

I rolled further down the window to let the wind in more and drown my thoughts with its sound. I looked outside and tried, in vain, to study the cloud formation, which was by then almost absent from the sky. I turned to look at Ashley. She's still asleep.

Why did I not bring a book?

I took my phone out of my bag. I had no roaming connection yet, so I contented myself by looking at the photographs taken from my recent trip to England. I was scared that if I looked at those photos from Egypt, my mind would delve into the dream again. Absent-mindedly, I was swiping through the album's contents, and when I saw those I took from the British Museum, I was taken aback upon seeing those artifacts from Egypt. I closed the phone abruptly. I closed my eyes and was rocking myself softly on my seat. The dream was forcing itself into my consciousness. Perhaps it's trying to tell me something. I tried to think then, but its meaning escaped me. I was growing frustrated when I chanced upon a civilization ahead. I asked the driver, and he confirmed my guess. We were approaching Petra.

We arrived just a short while before the sunset. We decided to take a walk around the neighborhood surrounding our hotel. There seemed to be more land than houses. I noticed as well that they didn't change their natural landscapes. Their houses were built either on the flat lands, by the hillsides, or on top of it. They adjusted to their natural surroundings instead of changing nature to suit their needs. When we went inside the heritage site the following morning, I was made to understand better why it was so.

The flight and the land travel made us both weary, so we both opted to stay in the room just right after our dinner at the nearby restaurant. We received an invitation for drinks on the rooftop from fellow tourists. I wanted to accept. I loved meeting new people and learning about their stories. But Ashley wasn't up to it so we passed up.

Upon reaching our room, we both got busy with our phones. I sent a message to Zaki to ask how he was. There's no reply until almost an hour later.

Zaki: I'm alright, Hanna. My meetings are exhausting. My mind is always tired. I miss you. How are you?

If only I could send myself along with my message. I missed being in Zaki's arms. I missed its warmth and comfort. What I wouldn't give to be with him right now.

Me: I'm okay. I'm missing you too, quite terribly. When are you back?
Zaki: After my meetings here in Oman, I'll be back in Dubai for some weeks. My passport would be up for renewal. I'm looking forward to being with you.

Zaki. Every part of me ached for him. How could a love like ours not be allowed to continue, to flourish, to reach greater heights? *Unless you become a Muslim yourself, you'll never be completely at one with him.* My sister-in-law's words stung like a scorpion's venom, working their way slowly to my heart.

"I thought love was the only unifying force."

"What's that, babe?"

I didn't realize I said that loud enough for Ashley to hear.

"I'm just thinking out loud. Don't mind me, babe."

"You seem to be in deep thoughts. Do you want to talk?"

"Would you ever consider marrying outside of your faith?" I asked as I turned on my side to face her.

"I have considered it. The adjustments between parties would be too much and might cause issues, so I have decided against the idea. Hinduism is not an easy religion to understand."

"Is there a religion that's easy to understand to begin with?"

"Precisely. That's why I have decided to stick to my own. Relationships alone can be hard. To have religion complicate it would be too much."

Ashley made a lot of sense. If religion were to be taken out of the equation, Zaki and I would be perfect. But our beliefs were central to the formation of our characters. I couldn't be certain that I would still have fallen in love with him had he not been a Muslim.

There's something so loose about the way Christian men have treated or observed their religion. It's something that troubled me, though I had never dared admit it openly. Not that I would prefer a deeply religious man. But spirituality should be an important aspect of anyone's life, whether we care to recognize it or not.

My phone vibrated on the bedside table, interrupting my line of thoughts.

> **Zaki**: I'm thinking about you. I have emails to answer, but I can't get myself to concentrate. You're persisting in my mind.
> **Me**: So are you in mine.
> **Zaki**: What are you thinking about exactly?
> **Me**: How perfect our love is, but there's this thick, clear Glass between us called religion that prevents us from being together.
> **Zaki**: It saddens me just as much, Hanna. But I don't Regret being a Muslim. If at the time of my birth, I had been given a chance to choose which religion to practice, I know I would still choose to be a Muslim.

I dashed out of bed and went to the bathroom. I made sure to lock the door so as not to worry Ashley should she accidentally walk in and found me crying.

I didn't feel an ounce of anger with Zaki's pronouncement of his faith. In fact, I felt my love for him had deepened a little bit more with that utterance. *Oh, Zaki, my love.* And my tears freely flowed.

Me: I would not wish for you to be anything else as well. I'm very proud of who you are. I feel privileged to have met you, Zaki. You're an amazing man.

I love you. I love you so much, Zaki.

More tears came. I felt my chest tightening as I tried to stifle my cry so as not to create any sound that could alert Ashley. I realized that even to my closest friends, I couldn't explain the intricacies of our situation or detail my pain. Our decision to honor the wishes of our families at the expense of our own happiness wasn't something the world of today could readily understand.

Zaki: If our circumstances had been different, I would Have married you from the start, Hanna. But I'm bound by tradition, and my faith demands my loyalty. Please know that it's futile for me to fight for you, knowing too well in the long run that you might still get hurt. And I can't afford that. I will put myself on the line, if I have to, to spare you from pain.

I had to cover my mouth as I howled because of the pain from within me. I had never felt so broken. I waited for him all my life, only to let him go after finding him. What a cruel joke fate had played on me! I tried to think of any offenses I might have made against anyone or any grievous sin I had committed to deserve this. My phone buzzed with another message from Zaki, interrupting my self-pity.

Zaki: I can hear your cry, Hanna. I can feel your tears in My heart.

His message pulled all the cords inside my heart. I had to pacify myself in order to respond. Few deep breaths before I managed to hold the phone again.

Me: I have waited for you for so long, Zaki. I can't just let you go now when all of me wants to stay with you.
Zaki: I'm just as confused and lost as you are, Hanna. Knowing you're hurting because of me makes me sick inside. If I could have one wish, it would be for you not to have met me. I would rather miss the opportunity of meeting an exceptional girl like you than be the cause of your suffering now.

His message caused me temporary paralysis, emotionally speaking. I understood what he meant to say. It was the thought of not meeting him which I found unbearable.

Me: Even if all hell breaks loose, I wouldn't wish not to have met you. You're worth it all, Zaki. Ours is a once-in-a-lifetime kind of love. If I were given the chance to

relive everything, even with the certainty of pain, I would still choose to love you.
Zaki: And so would I, Hanna.

*

Ashley set the alarm for eight, but I was up earlier. I had showered already and was watching a video about Petra when she took her turn. After breakfast, we crossed the street to the heritage site.

I composed myself properly so as not to give away anything that transpired last night. I didn't want to spoil the fun for Ashley, nor did I want to miss the magic of the experience of being there.

The documentary I watched earlier spoke with a tone of mystery and awe about an ancient group of people, called the Nabateaens, who built this wonderland with their bare hands and primitive, yet ingenious, tools. There were debates about its original purpose. Some archaeologists believed that those structures were tombs or sacred places, as explained by the Aramaic inscriptions on some facades. As we explored the complex, I realized that could be true. But on the other hand, I was baffled as to why there were no other remains or signs to indicate how some of those structures were actually used.

As we continued the walk, I was beginning to get the impression that this place might be more than a repository for their dead. There were huge blocks of rocks carved to make them look like columns. There were also human figures carved on the rock walls. Maybe a civilization also lived here, even though there were very few remains of their lives.

One of the first structures before reaching the Siq (the entranceway) was a building with a row of obelisks carved on top of what looked like a door and two other openings on either side. I took a peek inside. It was empty, but there were two sections of separated spaces in it and seemingly a welcome area in the middle. If it was a house, it certainly was an elegant one back then, what with the carved obelisks outside it. Then I remembered that in the video it was said that these structures were carved carefully in alignment with the sun's rays. From the same video, it's clear that the rays of the sun fell on the left side of the city. So I made an amateur assessment that perhaps that first structure was a sacred place of sorts and not a normal house. I walked a little to the right edge of the structure, and I noticed carved stairs. I didn't bother to go up to confirm my thoughts. The sun was intensifying, so we had to continue the walk.

Ashley was consumed with taking pictures, and I, with the video playing and pausing in my mind, was absorbed in understanding the mesmerizing beauty of this place. Some men on donkeys approached us and offered the services of their animals. We refused. No better way to immerse oneself in the beauty before us than by walking.

When we saw the towering cliffs covering the gorge leading to Petra proper, my heart started to pound double with excitement. I love exploring very old and ancient sites. It's like walking back in history, living the experiences of those who came before us. There were other carved structures along the way which, to me, resembled the house of the Flintstones, but no closures for the doorways, and all appeared similar to one another. When we reached the opening of the Siq, we took a few photos and went about our way. I noticed how flat and seamless the ground street was. According to the video, this was caused by nature – flood particularly. Petra was one of the driest areas on earth. To imagine it submerged in flood water was a little challenging, though close inspections of the rocks, one would be able to confirm that. There were outlined remnants of water evident on its façade, and when you touched it, you would know it had encountered water. I grew up in a city in the Philippines which had experienced some of the worst floods in our country's history. After the water had subsided and we were allowed to go outside, I had noted how slippery the rocks in our neighborhood were – my knees bore record of it. And the appearances of the stones were different than before the flood came. But again, that was just from my rudimentary understanding of nature.

The street was sandwiched between cliffs that were high enough to strain my neck. I paid close attention to the appearance of the sandstones. It showed marks of erosion. When I watched other videos about Petra after our visit, I affirmed this fact. When the site was opened to tourists, the degradation of the sandstones became drastic. Human contact could speed up the abasement of ancient artifacts for which the whole of Petra was. Museums in Egypt were very strict about visitors touching anything on display, as this could affect the decaying state of the item.

The mere thought of Egypt flashed Zaki into my consciousness. I took my phone out and checked the time. It's half past the hour of nine, local time. Zaki was in Oman, an hour ahead in timing from Jordan. I wondered what he was doing. The sound of an approaching horse brought me back to Petra. Ashley and I continued walking. I willed myself to be there and to be present at that moment.

When Ashley asked me to lean against the side of the cliff for a photograph, I finally noticed the canals the Nabataeans had built to irrigate the entire city. It was explained in the documentary that the source of their water was Ain Musa, some five miles away from Petra.

When the image of the Treasury started to come into view between the cliffs, we giggled like excited teenagers. As one continued to walk toward it, the imposing cliffs dissipated on the sides of your eyes, like curtains being parted, and the beautifully carved structure of the Treasury came into full view. It's an awesome sight to behold. I had seen in the documentary the intricate designs on top of its massive columns, so looking at it from the ground on actual helped me appreciate it fully. The Treasury had amazing carvings which spoke of varied influences from other countries. Up close or from afar, one could tell how smooth the finished exteriors were. Considering that they had limited resources then, especially in Petra, where I learned even wood was a scarcity, what they had achieved in creating this structure alone was immensely incredible. My thoughts flew to Zaki. I was wishing in my heart that he was seeing this with me. Indeed, when we loved someone, they permeated our every thought.

The heat was becoming a bit uncomfortable for me by the hour. Ashley was beginning to be weary. Just after we passed the Streets of Facades, she expressed an unwillingness to go on. She took shelter at the shop selling frankincense. I continued the exploration myself.

I went up to the Royal Tombs. It's an easy climb, but the heat made it somehow a challenge. Once I got on the top, though, it gave me a good view of everything that was below and the adjacent low mountains in the area.

The Urn Tomb was the first to greet visitors. It boasted high porticoes on either side of its façade, which I thought was reminiscent of Greek influence. The book I purchased about Petra after the visit confirmed that guess. This structure was believed to have been built as a burial for kings, though my amateur eyes couldn't readily accept that. I failed to find any indication that the place did serve that grand purpose. But then I thought maybe the monarchy of Jordan decided to transfer the royal remains when they opened the site to the public. Next to it was the Silk Tomb, so called because of the appearance of the bright-colored minerals that made up its rock. It had an amazing pattern across its body. It looked pinkish under the sun. The Corinthian Tomb had similar designs to that of the Monastery, though the latter seemed to have been better preserved. The Corinthian Tomb bore the marks of time. It could be compared to an old lady whose face had wrinkled but had managed to retain its beauty somehow. The Palace Tomb next to it was the same. But the creative, talented hands of those who carved it were still very visible to this day, aged but beautiful nonetheless.

I walked back to the Urn Tomb and took shelter from the sun for some minutes. My mind was beginning to wander back in time to when this place was still inhabited. Petra was in the direct path of the Silk Roads. The passersby from different parts of the world taking the Silk Roads to trade their goods must have been mesmerized by the extraordinary beauty of this city. If I was enchanted by its charm and beauty now, with all that's remained of it, I was certain more so those who came before me thousands of years back.

When I returned to Ashley, she was in deep conversation with the shop owner, who was a strikingly good-looking man.

I wanted to sit down with them, but there was still much to see. So Ashley and I agreed to meet at the hotel around lunchtime. I hired a horse to cover the remaining area faster.

I was taking photos as I rode along without needing to get off the horse. Those carved structures have nothing inside them now. The façades really were all there was to see. I had my head fully covered to protect me from the sun. I only had my eyes exposed, shaded by my sunglasses. I was thinking to myself, *It's not so bad to be well covered after all.* Then the dream on the plane came back to me at once. As if it's just waiting for its queue to come out to torment me. I gently kicked the horse on the side to will it to run faster. That way I was forced to concentrate on something else, like balancing myself properly for one, or I could topple over.

As the horse and I strode along the Colonnaded Street, I saw ruins of what looked to me where columns and structures typical of Roman architecture. When I reached the Nymphaeum, which I had learned was an area in the city dedicated to nymphs and water, and down to the Great Temple and auditorium, I noticed immediately the marks of colonization. Humans had always been captivated by beauty, regardless in what form, and we could not simply just allow it to be. It seemed innate in us to possess whatever it may be that held our attention and marked it as our own. As I surmised in the book I bought, I realized that as Petra prospered, it became more beautiful. Its own beauty contributed to its downfall.

As I continued along, my longing to have Zaki with me on that trip was growing. It would have been nice to exchange views with him about this place. I knew he would have loved to see this too. This place was built out of the great love the

Nabataeans had for their culture and traditions. I lacked the skill to carve or paint. I could weave words beautifully together in poems, though. But words lose their depth after some time. With distance, all of it would eventually be just that: words. This thought saddened me. I didn't want Zaki to forget me. I was certain I would never forget him. How could I? How could the heart forget the very reason it was beating for?

I was worn out and starving by the time I reached the Monastery at the end of the complex. But I was temporarily taken in by the magnificence of the sight before me. The Monastery seemed bigger than the Treasury, but the craftsmanship was the same. These masterpieces from Petra were unlike anything else in the world. Time and the ravages of nature didn't do much harm to the extraordinary beauty of this place.

After snapping some pictures, I took my leave. I made the horse run a bit faster to reach the hotel quicker. Mid-way all too suddenly, almost like a vision, an image came into my mind, and it grew bigger by the second that I had to stop the horse. With eyes wide open, I saw a giant me towering over the pyramids, my raven hair getting tangled with the white clouds. I looked down and saw myself burning alive and my tears seemingly fueling the fire. Violently, I shook my head, willing for the vision to end. The lad from whom I rented the horse was looking at me with bewilderment. I told him I was alright, and I resumed the ride. I silently resolved to review my dreams after I had lunch.

Ashley was waiting for me in the hotel's restaurant when I got back. Despite the earlier hunger I felt, I couldn't eat as much. There seemed like a volcano inside my heart that was going to explode any minute. Ashley noticed my uneasiness. I reasoned with her that I was just tired.

Upon reaching our room, I headed straight into the bathroom. I wouldn't use the bathtubs in hotels if I could help it, but I felt like soaking myself completely in water then. It could be because I was subconsciously hoping it could cool down the lava ready to spill out from within me.

When the tub filled up, I got into it. Water had a way of relaxing me, regardless of what I could be going through at any given time. Just after some minutes, I felt my tensions slackening. I closed my eyes and intentionally thought of the dreams I had.

Egypt is a predominantly Muslim country now. But the pyramids were still its foremost identifying feature. My dream to see the pyramids had started at a tender age. So was my desire to meet my ideal man. Both came true in a simultaneous fashion, so to speak. I would have loved to live in Egypt and be close to the pyramids and their many ancient wonders. But unless I could find a job there, it would be impossible for me to stay longer than 30 days. Marriage to an Egyptian would be the only other viable option. I would not have anyone else except Zaki. The depth of my love for him produced the same amount of pain, consuming me like fire, burning me to the ground completely.

The second dream was a premonition of sorts in itself. It would take more than wearing an abaya to be fully converted to the Muslim faith. I could learn more about Islam and its prayers and core practices, but the changes it could bring into my life could shift my internal balance, causing me to lose my footing and perhaps eventually fall down in confusion and despair. I had to let go of Zaki. Ours may be a beautiful love, one worthy of being written about, but it could bring about my own destruction.

Tears came, plenty and fast. I could fill the tub with it alone. The immense pain I was feeling was drowning me and pulling me out on all sides at the same time. How could love hurt this much? *Zaki*. I hugged my legs and cried on my knees. Thinking that he might be experiencing the same thing hurt me twice over. We're two people who loved each other and wanted to be together. What was the sense of this pain?

Chapter 7

November 2016

"The end is coming. What are you going to do with the time you have left?" As if Mitch Albom wrote those words especially for me. My dear friend Melka gifted me a copy of The Timekeeper, one of the author's best-selling works. She's not much of a reader, despite working in the biggest bookstore in the UAE, but she had good taste when choosing what to give me.

"There's been a good demand for that one, though not new. So I thought perhaps you would like it as well," Melka said when she handed me the book over dinner one Thursday night.

"Mitch Albom is a very good writer. He has thought-provoking works. Thank you for this. I'll start on it this weekend."

"You need to go out and not sulk at home. Solitude can only intensify your sadness."

"I'm not really up to going anywhere. Besides, this one really seems like a good read. You know how I am when it comes to a new book." I try to put as much enthusiasm into my tone when speaking with my friends, though I knew I was not fooling any of them regardless. But I was thankful that none of them pressed on me any further.

"Babe, if you need someone to talk to, I'm just a call away. Don't forget that. And I'm sorry I can't be with you on your birthday." Melka gave me a tight hug before allowing me to get out of her car.

My friends had been doubly concerned and were extra sensitive in their communications with me since learning of my emotional predicament. I welcomed all their attention and pampering, as it worked like balm on my shattered heart.

Zaki and I had maintained our close friendship. The certainty of the end was looming larger before us as the days went on. His move to our France office had already been decided to be in January of the following year. We just rolled into November, and my birthday would be in two weeks' time, the last that we could celebrate together. Tears were always at the ready, even with the slightest trigger of memory. In less than a minute, my cheeks were saturated with it. For the first time in my life I didn't want to let go. For the first time in my life I didn't want to be left behind. For the first time in my life I couldn't imagine living without someone. I picked up my phone and sent him a message on WhatsApp.

Me: What I wouldn't give to keep you.

His response was quick. I was just about to put down my phone on my study table when it vibrated again.

Zaki: I have the same thought every day, Hanna. But I can't bend my principles, even for love. Neither do I want you to consider the same.

I cried a bit more after having read his message. I felt betrayed by life. *What have I done to deserve this?* I sobbed hard against my pillow, soaking it in the process. My phone vibrated on the table again. It was Zaki calling. I accepted the call, but I couldn't word anything out.

"It's just as hard and painful for me, Hanna. You're important to me. I care about you so much. I wish there was something else I could do."

Every word registered to me along with the emotion it came with, serving only to intensify mine own. It took me some time to respond.

"It's not fair," I wanted to say more, but words and emotions clogged my throat, disabling my tongue. I continued to sob.

"Every drop of your tears is a pin pinch through my heart."

"Zaki."

"Hanna. My Hanna. I'm so sorry," I heard his voice cracked. I felt a force stabbing me from within. I willed myself to say something, but no words would come out. My emotions were too high then.

"I'm flying back tomorrow. Our work here in Saudi Arabia is over. Let's see each other tomorrow, okay?" Deep sadness was evident in his voice, but he tried to sound optimistic for whatever little our diminishing time together could offer.

"Alright. I'll wait for you tomorrow, then," I managed to choke out those words, though I wasn't sure if he understood.

"Until tomorrow, then. Try to get some rest now. I'm holding you in my heart."

"And you in mine." Seconds after, I pressed on the red telephone icon, cutting off the call, but my heart was desperately clinging on to our connection.

"The end is coming. What are you going to do with the time you have left?" The words from the book haunted me from day to night. It's on auto-repeat in my head. I was feeling pressured, thinking that time was ticking away, yet I was paralyzed from doing anything.

*

When sleep came, it made me dream, which further compounded my longing upon waking up. Zaki was central to all of it. In one dream, we were in what looked like an apartment, and he was preparing something in the kitchen. At another time, we were swimming at JBR. After that we were enjoying ourselves with our colleagues over food and Karaoke. The scenes seemed interconnected and formed one long movie in my mind.

My phone vibrating on the study table interrupted my thoughts. It's a WhatsApp message from Zaki inviting me for lunch. I checked the time and immediately got off the bed. I had an hour to prepare myself.

While in the shower, a thought came to me, almost like a whispered secret. "*Make it count.*" I switched off the shower and stood perfectly still, thinking about it.

"Make it count," I repeated the words aloud. My heart began to beat with excitement. *I will make the remaining time count. I still have him. We still have time.*

I opened my cabinet doors and carefully scanned my dresses. To make an impact is important. Zaki had always remarked well about my legs. Winter was just starting, so I could still wear a short dress. I chose the dark blue one with sleeves right to the elbow. It hugged my figure right and gave maximum exposure to my shapely legs. I paired it with black ballerina flats and a black clutch. I thought it would be good to carry a shawl in case I needed to cover my legs if the temperature dropped come evening. I hardly wore makeup. A bold red lipstick had been my favorite statement when going out. But I didn't feel right to sport that color then. So I opted for a lighter touch of rose and two coats of mascara to open my Chinese eyes a little bit. I never experimented with hairstyles, and neither did I want to look too put together. So I just blow-dried it well and slightly curled the ends inward. "Au naturale", as Zaki would always say to me.

At 45 minutes after 11, he was calling me, always punctual, ever the gentleman.

"Hi, handsome. I'm ready."

"You always are, beautiful. I would be arriving in ten minutes."

The pleased look on his face when I stepped out of my building was an instant boost to my confidence. I was scoring well early on in the day, so to speak.

"You're looking mighty fine, Hanna." And he gave me a kiss on the forehead before opening the door of the car to usher me in.

"Thank you. You're equally handsome, as ever." I lightly ran my hand on his chest, making sure his body felt the message I was wishing to communicate. Then I got inside the car.

As he was driving out of my cluster, he mentioned that we were going to The Palm. I knew in an instant where exactly.

"Do we need to make a reservation at Anantara at this hour?"

"Perhaps not. We have not gone there during the day time, though. Do you want me to make the call now just to be sure?"

"I don't think there are a lot of people there now. Otherwise, we will just carry on somewhere. I hope that's okay with you."

"Anywhere is fine with me, Zaki, so long as we are together." I reached for his hand. I felt emotional again. *Make this day count.* I reminded myself. He squeezed my hand. I looked at him, and we smiled at each other, a smile that conveyed love and understanding.

"I missed you. How have you been?"

"I can wish for better days. But then others have had it worse. So I can't complain."

"How do you do that? How do you remain so composed and positive regardless of what is going on?"

"It's not my nature to be noisy, for one. And I'm a praying man, Hanna. In a world like we live in now, it matters, and it does wonders for one's life."

I reached out to touch his face. He kissed the back of my hand. Tears were knocking on my lids. I closed my eyes, and small drops escaped. I fished the handkerchief from my clutch bag.

"I don't like you crying, Hanna. It hits me at the core of my manhood, not knowing how to make those tears go away."

"Don't blame yourself for anything, Zaki. Neither of us wished for how things have turned out between us. And I'm sorry for displaying my emotions so openly like this. It's just that the pain is eating me away inside." I patted dry each of my cheeks, but tears kept both wet. Zaki stopped on the shoulder of the road.

"Hanna, look at me," he asked gently as he reached for my hand. "You don't apologize to me for crying. I'm not deserving of those tears. No man should make a woman cry. Yet, here you are, hurting because of me. What I would not do to…" He looked to the other side and then bowed his head. "I'm so sorry, Hanna. I'm so sorry." He started to sob.

"Zaki." He looked at me and there was deep sadness in his beautiful green eyes. I unbuckled myself and moved closer to him. He removed his eyeglasses and nestled his face on my neck, our arms wrapped around each other. I felt his tears on my skin, seemingly seeping through my pores, streaming down to my heart, and filling me with the sadness of his.

After some minutes, I moved a little away to look at his face. His eyes were still moist. I wiped it dry and I kissed his cheeks deeply, one after the other, and then his forehead. I wanted to say I loved him. But words were not necessary when your emotions were speaking for you.

"Should we go to Anantara now? I'm starving," I said with a smile. He composed himself and stepped on the accelerator.

The resort was crowded. But the happy vibe in the air obviously rubbed off well on everyone around. We were pleased to find a table at Crescendo, one of their restaurants that served international cuisine. We were seated inside, which was just alright since the view of each other was better than anything. Knowing full well just how long we had left, I wanted to look at him all the chance I got.

After our lunch, we walked to the beach area. Families with children were playing by the shore, while others were swimming in the pristine waters. I looked up at him, and with a smile, he came closer and pulled me to him, enwrapping me in his arms. He leaned his forehead against mine. I loved that moment. It was easily one of my most favorite times with him. He didn't say a word, but his actions made me understand the depth of his feelings for me. I leaned my head on his chest after a minute, with our arms still around each other. I felt him kiss me on the head. What I wouldn't give to stay in that moment, to not let it end.

"I love you," I murmured against his chest. I felt him move. I looked up at him and he was looking at me with an intensity I had never before seen in his eyes. Then, in a split second, he pressed his lips on mine, forcing me to open and accept him completely. It threw me off course, but I was more than willing to get lost in the moment. After what seemed like a minute, his lips left mine, enabling me to breathe. My heart was pounding, and my knees were weakening.

"I have wondered for years how it would feel to kiss your lips." He was looking at me with love and longing while running his thumb on my lower lip. I just smiled. I was still a bit disoriented to say anything. The kiss shook me inside but in a good way. It felt so different from what I had experienced before.

A true love's kiss.

"What are you thinking about?" He asked in a teasing voice.

"We've never kissed before. I've always wondered how it would be like when we finally do. You surprised me." I was certain I was blushing.

"I couldn't hold myself any longer. There have been so many times I wanted to do it. And this dress you're wearing…wow! I've not seen you in one like this before." The raw desire evident in his eyes prolonged the blushing of my cheeks.

"Thank you. It's from Lourdes. I thought it would be perfect for today."

"It is, and you look perfect in it." He leaned his forehead on mine again, but this time his lips reached down to kiss mine once more, just gently brushing them. I felt the movements of his lips as he said my name. It caused electric currents to run through my body, igniting further the passion already brewing inside me.

"I want to kiss you more and longer." It was almost like a whisper, but it reverberated loudly in my ears, sending waves of electricity down to my sex. I looked up at him with a smile, conveying my agreement to his unasked question. He understood and we started heading for the exit. He only let go of my hand when his car pulled into the driveway.

He didn't ask me, but neither did I need to be asked if he could take me back to his place. In all these years, I hadn't been to Zaki's apartment. We were practically neighbors, with just the Metro footbridge separating us, yet we hadn't been to each other's flats before. I was hesitant to walk in when he opened the door.

"I'm not used to going to a man's place. Please don't be offended by my initial hesitation."

"I figured that might be the case; that's why I've never extended the invitation until now."

I was standing by the kitchen counter, reluctant to move. My heart was beating faster and I felt moist down between my legs. He sensed my discomfort. He came over and enveloped me in his arms.

"Relax. It's just us now. You are home." And he kissed me on the lips again, gently at first, and it built momentum by the seconds. He was opening my mouth, asking me to take him in, while his arms had me locked to him. I was reciprocating his passion, pressing my body harder against his, making him aware of my own desires.

"Hanna," he said my name over and over between torrid kisses. He lifted me up on the counter and his lips hungrily rummaged my neck, pushing me to the edge of my arousal.

"Zaki…" I was starting to slightly convulse. I could feel a hot liquid starting to leave my body from my sex. "Zaki…" I pressed my legs together for fear that something might gust out of me.

He carried me to the bedroom and laid me down. He came on top of me and we started kissing again, this time a lot more intensely and deeper, heating us both even more. When his hand started to move downward, caressing my legs, I lost it. I felt my hot juice slide down my anus, soaking my panty. He knew what was happening to me. He slid my dress upward, exposing my panty and stomach. He inhaled deeply on my navel. I felt another ounce of hotness ready to come out of me. He pulled my dress off completely. He was staring at me with deep lust and hunger in his eyes while he was undressing himself. I was continuously coming.

"Zaki," my breathing was haggard, shallow and with a sense of profound hunger.

When his nakedness touched mine there was like a spark being exchanged by our bodies, traveling at such a speed from scalp to sole, lips to soul. Our mouths barely separated. We couldn't get enough of each other. There was a deep desire that was driving us both mad and excited and hungrier by the minute. Feeling his manhood growing and pressing hard on me intensified my arousal. Years of suppressed emotions and desires led to that moment.

But when he unclasped my bra, he suddenly froze. He just stopped moving. I couldn't move myself. I was afraid that if I did, or said anything, the whole thing would be over. His breathing was hard and fast, mirroring mine. Then he started to murmur against my ear. Until his words became audible.

"I cannot. I must not. This is wrong. I should not." I was listening to him in bewilderment. I still couldn't talk. The sudden shift of events perplexed me.

What's going on?

"I shouldn't be doing this to you. I shouldn't be doing this," he repeated himself a few more times and stood. He looked at me and walked toward the bathroom without saying a word.

I was trying to process in my mind what had just happened. I wanted to move and put my dress back on because I was feeling embarrassed. But all of me was paralyzed at that moment like I was nailed to the bed. When I heard the water from the shower hit the bathroom floor, I willed myself to get up. I didn't realize I was already crying. My movements were mechanical and my mind was in a daze.

I was sitting on the edge of the bed when he stepped out of the bathroom. I kept my head down. I was both embarrassed and hurt. I didn't understand why. Zaki sat down beside me. He was fully dressed, too.

"Hanna, I'm sorry. I lost control." I didn't respond. I couldn't. I felt his eyes on me. I kept my gaze downward. I felt like a paper bag being tossed back and forth by the wind. I was dizzy and started to feel sick. He knelt before me, holding my hands and forcing me to look at him.

"I don't have any rights to touch you, Hanna. No matter how deep my love goes for you, unless I marry you, I can't touch you. You mean so much to me. I can't afford to tarnish you with my desires. I'm sorry." He kissed my hands, then laid his face on my lap, curling his arms around my waist.

"There's nothing to apologize for. I understand. Perhaps I should be the one apologizing." He looked up at me with questioning eyes. "You know, for wearing this dress."

"No! You have the right to wear what suits you. What you're wearing is not an excuse for me to lose control. I'm the man." I cupped his face with my hands and gently kissed his lips.

"And what a man you are, Zaki. You're causing my bosom to expand with pride for you."

"And what a bosom you have, mademoiselle!" he said in a playful tone. We kissed again, subtle but still passionate. After, he proposed that we moved back to the living room. I didn't protest, knowing too well how much he was struggling to bridle his desires.

"Would you like tea?" I didn't realize how thirsty I was until he asked.

"A cup would be good. Thanks." I walked over to the window and saw for the first time the view of the Marina from that angle.

"It's very nice at night when all the lights are on. The place becomes sort of magical," he said as he approached with our tea.

"I know. When I walk going to JBR on some nights, I always stop by the bridge to look at this view. And I always stare at your apartment building with longing." He came over to me and embraced me from behind. As I felt his arms tighten around me, I closed my eyes to take in the moment.

Nothing can be better than this.

"Hanna." He turned my face to his and he invaded my mouth again. I was still as aroused so my lips instantly reacted. I kissed him with all the love I had been feeling for him all this time. I pulled him to me when he pushed me against the wall as if I was afraid that whatever it was that was building between us then would be deconstructed by the little distance that separated our bodies.

"Hanna." His breath was hot, evident of his reignited passion. It deepened mine own, causing me to be so wet again, almost to the brink of climax. He lifted me up and he sat on the sofa, with me on his lap still feasting on his lips. His hands were slowly running up and down my legs, which encased his, lifting my dress dangerously high in the process. His lips came down on my neck and I was once more entirely lost in the moment. Our tea had gone cold while we both got heated up again.

We spent the afternoon kissing and cuddled intimately on the small space of his couch. We stayed outside the bedroom the entire time. Three movies had started and ended, one after the other, but we barely followed any one of them. There's that very strong magnetic force pulling our lips to each other all the time. At one point, he saw my juice come out of me, sliding down one thigh while I slightly trembled. He rose to walk to the bathroom with a bulging erection to get me tissues. He wiped me dry, his hand so dangerously close to my sex. After which, he walked back to the bathroom and didn't come out right away. I heard the shower again. *He's trying to douse his erection with cold water.* I felt sad about it. He couldn't express his love for me fully. His body was struggling to contain his overwhelming feelings. When he came out, I stood and embraced him, with my own emotions ready to spill out.

"Perhaps I should go now. I'm causing you so much discomfort."

"No! Don't worry about me. It's alright. No, stay Hanna, please. I don't want you to go." He was holding me so tight, proving to me the sincerity of what he said.

"I love being in your arms. You're my most favorite place, Zaki."

"I thought it was Egypt," he said jokingly.

"You are Egypt. You are England. You are the world to me, Zaki." I didn't want to ruin the moment, but my tears just came out without warning. I buried my face in his chest. I felt his arms tighten a bit around me.

"You're just the sweetest, Hanna. I have never had anyone like you before. The feeling you awakened in me, I never knew I could feel this way for anyone."

"Why can't we stay like this for all our lives?" The tears couldn't be helped. If it's the heart crying, it could not be stopped.

"I want you to be mine completely. I want you to be my wife. I want you to carry my name. I want you to introduce me to everyone in your life as your husband. I want all of it, Hanna. I want to live my life with you. But we are not the only two people in this world. We have our families and relatives, and there's religion to consider," he stopped talking. I chose not to interrupt the silence. I tried to ponder on his words instead.

"I wanted to ready the apartment for us back in May. I told my mother about you when I asked for the key. We had an argument, so I left the house, took the train to Cairo, and waited for you there, scouting for a good hotel to book you at. I felt guilty. She's my mother. It was Eid. So I had to leave you alone in the hotel that night." I wasn't surprised by his admission. I knew something had happened. It wasn't like Zaki to change what had been planned at the last minute. He's a calculated man, never leaving anything to chance, especially if it concerns me or his team.

"I don't want you to convert to Islam just because of me. You're an intelligent lady. You have a very good understanding of my faith. But Islam is different in practice and in theory, Hanna. I'll be here to support you and help you understand it more. But I feel like I would be betraying my own heart even by merely asking you to consider conversion. I love you for what you are, what you believe in, and all. I don't want to change anything about you. What guarantee do I have that you will become a far better person than how you are now when you become a Muslim? I don't believe religion is the only factor that makes a person who they are. There's so much more. But I belong to a family that has observed the Muslim faith for ages. I'm the only son of my parents. I can't break our tradition. Well, I can, but that will mean breaking my family's hearts and those of our clan. It's a tough life ahead, Hanna. I don't think you deserve to go through all those hardships just for me." A tear slid down his cheek. I reached up to his face to wipe it with my thumb, my own eyes still wet.

"I love you, Hanna. Letting you go would break my heart, but it's also the greatest manifestation of my love for you." He fell down on his knees in front of me and hugged my legs while crying. I cried even harder. My heart felt like exploding. I attempted to kneel down, but my strength gave way, and I found myself on the floor, crashed and utterly vulnerable. He took me in his arms and we cried together for some time. No one had cried for me before. Well, none that I knew of. So seeing Zaki crying like that because of me was squeezing my heart to the brink of combustion.

After some time, we dried each other's eyes.

"Tough love, huh?" I said jokingly.

"I wouldn't wish for it to be anything else, Hanna. Tough love or what, you are worth it. Just that…" I put a finger against his lips.

"It's alright. I understand completely. I wouldn't want you to suffer so much while defending me from your family. They are your flesh and blood. They are you. If they get hurt because of you choosing me, I will also hurt you in the process. We're going to begin an unending cycle of pain that might affect our children down through time. Peace would be elusive. What's love without peace? I love you, Zaki, like I had never loved anyone before you. It's hurting me terribly to let you go. But love is not the only thing we have in this life. Love can't bypass or set aside age-old traditions that have shaped us and our families. Love cannot…" I couldn't continue. My tongue was stopped by my tears, so to speak. He held me closer to him, gently rocking both of us as a way to soothe the ache eating us both inside.

I woke up with a start and my legs were feeling cold. Zaki moaned when he sensed my movement. We fell asleep on the floor. I couldn't tell what time it was. But it's already dark. I couldn't move so much. Zaki's arms were around me. I looked at him and examined his face. I wondered if he was dreaming and of what. I laid my hand on his cheek and gently caressed it. I ran my thumb over his lips. My emotions were getting stirred again. *What would I become without you?* Tears were threatening to come again. I moved closer to him until our foreheads were touching.

"I love you," I whispered to him. He pulled me closer to him. Our lips found each other again. Soft kisses at first, then it quickly picked up its pace as our bodies were being woken up with desires. Without a thought, I moved one leg to angle my body properly to him. But I ended up hitting his erection. He growled softly. I muttered an apology in between kisses. He joked that I only made it angrier. I giggled.

"Oh, Hanna, your innocence is weakening me." He kissed me again, ever so softly. It's an overwhelming kind of kiss, filling me up to the brim, so to speak. Yet I wanted more. But I worried that the night might make us do something more.

"It's dark now. Perhaps I should go," I said it, ever so gently, so as not to cross him. He raised his eyes to mine and invaded my lips without a preamble. He slowly moved on top of me, pinning me completely to the floor. Our lips wouldn't part. Zaki's weight was pressing me harder against the cold floor. I had him completely wrapped in both arms and legs. I had never before kissed anyone that long, lips and tongue deeply engaged as if we wanted to get inside each other. Then he suddenly stopped, started shaking, and gave out a soft growl. For a moment I was alarmed, but then I felt damp where our sexes met. I held him tighter as he emptied himself.

"Let me clean myself," he said, rather embarrassed, as he slowly lifted his face to look at me. I just smiled at him; certain I was blushing.

"The way you're looking at me now, Hanna, you're making it impossible for me to let you go home tonight." I failed to stifle my laughter. Instead of standing up, he rolled to my side and started laughing too. I looked at his soaked pants and laughed even harder. His entire front was wet!

"That's a lot! You look like as though a bottle of mineral water has been spilled on you!"

"Yes, it felt that way, only it's sticky!" And his laughter filled the apartment and my heart. I rolled to his side and gave him soft kisses on his jaw. When I reached his lips, I planted light kisses on them too.

"Don't go, Hanna. Stay with me tonight." His beautiful green eyes were pleading at me so sweetly.

"Will I not push you over the edge by staying?"

"You just did. And I'm sure it will be repeated two or three times more during the course of the night. But I'll make sure not to touch you beyond my right to do so." I rolled off him and flattened my back straight against the floor. Its coldness made me shake inside out. Zaki noticed it.

"Of course, if you're not comfortable, it's alright. Let me clean my – "

"I would love to stay here. I would love to remain this close to you, Zaki. But I don't want to cause you any discomfort, and I don't want to be tempted beyond my threshold…again." I put as much weight on my voice as possible to stress my last point.

"Hanna, I'm sorry. I didn't know – " Zaki's voice was loaded with alarm and concern.

"No need to apologize, Zaki. I'm taking no offense. None of these are offensive. All I'm saying is we need to be careful."

"You're right, mademoiselle. I'm doing a poor job handling this situation. Your presence disorients me, Hanna, in a positive way, though." He kissed me on the right cheek before standing, then offered to help me get up. His lips were on mine again the moment I was standing opposite him. I welcomed the intrusion and returned his passion with as much ardor. But he pulled away before the kiss got too intense again. When he walked toward the bedroom, I didn't stop him.

I went to the guests' washroom opposite the kitchen to wipe myself dry. My body's behaving wildly today. While inside, there was a debate waging in my head about whether I should stay over for the night or not. I was confused but happy. Soft knocks on the door jolted me out of my thoughts. I steeled myself inside when he turned the knob. I didn't realize I hadn't locked the door. Had he come in a moment earlier, he would have found me in a compromising position. We were looking at each other in the mirror.

"Why are you holding yourself up in here?" he teasingly said, cocooning me in his arms. I felt his warm breath on my neck. I closed my eyes and allowed his presence to fully invade me. When I faced him, his lips were ready and obviously eager to take mine. I couldn't will myself to pull away. His kisses were highly addictive. His touches burned my skin and caused my passion to bloom in flames. If it were possible to melt and be absorbed into him, or he into me, we would have become as one matter together that moment.

"Please stay, Hanna, stay with me." When it's another heart making a plea, how could you not give heed?

"Alright, I will stay." He hugged me tightly and I felt the excited throbbing of his heart against my breast.

*

We decided to go to JBR for dinner. Zaki didn't know how to cook, and neither did I. Walking hand in hand, and talking heart to heart, I had never been as happy and proud as when I was with him. Falling in love with each other was like an achievement on its own that I wanted to show off to the world.

We had to stop at a crossing point to give way for the tram to pass. He brought my hand to his lips. We had always been calculated with our actions in public. Today, his gestures surprised me. I looked up at him with crimson cheeks and a smile that emanated from my heart. He winked at me and draped one arm over my shoulders. I snuggled closer to him as we continued the walk.

JBR never failed to draw in the crowd, especially during the weekend. But before leaving his place we had already decided to go to The Cheesecake Factory. It was nearly full, but there was still one table left for us on the first floor. The cozy, dim interior and the noise from other diners made it perfect for us to sit together very close. Feeling the tip of his nose on my cheek made me feel dreamy. I wished every night to be like that.

"I'd pay 100 Dirhams just to know what you're thinking, Hanna."

"Money down and I'll tell you."

"Smart girl!" I offered my lips and he readily took it. He planted light kisses on me and caressed my nose with that of his.

"I have never felt this full and happy. You're amazing, Habibi."

"And so are you, my Hanna. I love you."

Our tender moment was interrupted when the waiter approached our table for our orders. Shortly afterward, our attention was back to each other. We spoke of work and the goings-on in the office for some time before he mentioned my birthday.

"How would you like to celebrate it?"

"Every day is a celebration on its own if we're together," My voice couldn't hide the sadness that was inside me.

"You know I'm willing to do whatever it takes for that to be possible. But I can't guarantee that in our pursuit of our happiness there will be no pain along the way. And you getting hurt is not something I can afford."

I fell more deeply in love with Zaki that night. But the pain of losing him intensified as well. I reached for his hand and caressed it with both of mine.

"I haven't come up with any plans as yet. Maybe we can just have dinner again." My mind had been preoccupied with counting the days when he would be transferred that I forgot even my own birthday.

"There's something weighing on your mind, Hanna. You know you can talk to me about anything."

I couldn't know then if there would be any man again who could look at me in the same way he did and be able to see my rumbling thoughts through my face.

"Zaki, I don't think it's a good idea for me to stay with you tonight." I wanted to say more and defend my stand so as to make him understand that it's not a refusal or rejection, but more of a fear on my end for the inevitable. But I was worried I might complicate the moment. Zaki was quiet, and oddly enough, the world seemed to be so too in that instance. I looked at him and saw both sadness and confusion in his eyes.

"Zaki, I've not slept with any man. You have my heart, and I think you will always be in it. I know I can't stop loving you. I know I'll never forget you. Everything might become more difficult for me after, if ever."

"Hanna, I would not dare…"

"We almost had, Zaki. We almost did it. The night is a treacherous time. What if I failed to restrain myself? I'm certain you wouldn't be able to refuse me. Please Zaki…" He released his hand from my grasp and took me in his arms.

"I understand what you're telling me. You're right. I'm sorry to have overlooked that thought. I'm overwhelmed. I'm torn inside. I'm a basket of confusion right now, Hanna. Forgive me." He pressed his lips hard on my forehead. My heart felt the sincerity of that act.

Our orders came and the waiter was reluctant to approach, seeing us that way. Zaki motioned him to come forward and he proceeded to place our food on the table. We kissed lightly on the lips before disentangling from each other.

We passed the time talking about his imminent move and new role once he transferred, while commenting now and again about our dinner. He was obviously excited about the change he was to embark on. It was painful for me to listen to him. But I loved him enough not to stand in the way of his dreams and professional growth.

We strolled by the shore shortly after finishing our dinner, talking about random things like the weather as we went along. This place held a special place in my memory, for it's here where Zaki first vocalized his feelings for me. The sea was rushing fast to the shore same as the emotions wildly barraging the walls of my heart. I looked up and found the moon slowly hiding behind the clouds. Even it at that moment didn't want to witness the tragedy of two hearts being forced by life to separate.

*

A simple card and a small black elephant figurine were on our table when we got there. As soon as I was helped to my seat, five staff members came with a slice of cake and sang me a happy birthday. Zaki was taking the video. Tears escaped my eyes while making a wish. He stopped recording and came to me. I rose from my seat and buried my face in his neck. Then, momentarily, I heard thundering claps. I looked in the direction of the sound and was surprised to see our whole team standing in front of us. Zaki had me blindfolded the moment we reached the lobby entrance of the Anantara Hotel in The Palm. He helped me get all the way through to our table at the Mekong Restaurant. I didn't have time to feel embarrassed because they started singing their greeting for me. Roshie handed Zaki a bouquet of white roses when they finished. I was overwhelmed. When I had thanked each one of them, they went back inside the restaurant, where a bigger table was set up for them. The two of us stayed outside on our rickshaw seats.

"That's very sweet and sneaky of you to do, Zaki. So much for a simple dinner, huh?" I said it jokingly.

"You don't deserve simple, Hanna. I would have invited the whole world here had it been possible."

"My whole world is right in front of me now. I couldn't ask for anything more."

"Neither could I, Habibi." And he reached for my hand across the table only to place it on top of a red box, which I hadn't noticed was there earlier. "Happy birthday, Hanna!"

"Zaki! What is this?"

"Open it."

A gold necklace with a crescent moon pendant shone before my eyes. All the words escaped me. My eyes expressed what my lips failed to say. I couldn't move, and so Zaki came to my side and took the necklace from its box. I straightened my posture as he placed the gift on my neck. It was the perfect length, with the pendant reaching just the top of my cleavage. He knelt beside me and kissed me on the right cheek.

"To remind you that I'll always be close to you at heart. I love you so much, Hanna."

I kissed him full on the lips, my tears dampening his cheeks in the process. He answered me with as much gusto. Our lips were forced to separate when we heard cheers from inside. I forgot that our entire office, with the exception of the boss, was there too. Zaki rose to his feet and went back to his seat. We joined our team for the main course. There were two seats ready for us. Zaki had planned the evening well. It's the happiest celebration in my recent memory.

After dinner we decided to hang around the sea area in front of the Atlantis Hotel. The weather was very pleasant, with a slight cool breeze. I handed Zaki a gift I wrapped in satin red cloth.

"Hanna, it's not my birthday." He pulled me closer to him as he accepted my present. I tiptoed to reach his lips for a quick kiss.

"Open it."

"An iPhone watch! Hanna…"

"To remind you of a time when someone loved you so much, enough to let you go."

We embraced and didn't separate until after some time. Then we stood in silence, side by side, looking out to the sea. We had emptied our minds of things to say to each other. There's nothing left to be said. No words could make anything work in our favor. In my heart there was just immense love and respect and harrowing sadness left.

I turned around and looked at the Atlantis Hotel. He copied my movement. He seemed as lost as I was.

"Do you think the legend of Atlantis is true?" I asked him.

"I don't know. But I know my love for you is." He's looking at me with both pride and sadness in his eyes. I came closer to him and wrapped my arms around his neck.

"If there's a chance for us in another life, would you love me again?"

"Yes, and even in another life after that, Zaki." We kissed with all the love that we felt for each other. We would stop only for some air and to look at each other. Our lips would reconnect only with much stronger desire each time.

The area was deserted. The sea was quiet. Hardly was there any ongoing traffic as well. As if we were being allowed by fate to have that moment. The moon was high up in the night sky, the only witness of our passion, bearing a record of the promises exchanged by two hearts pulled in by love but being forced by life to be apart.

You had never really loved
until you learned to let go.
You had never really loved
until you could understand
without reason or explanation.
You had never really loved
until words failed to describe
what you felt
and the world failed
to measure the depth
of your feelings.

***

Han Birondo